THE WITCH OF APPALACHIA

Book 1
The Wolf Master of Iron Mountain

Francesca Quarto

THE WITCH OF APPALACHIA
Book 1 - The Wolf Master of Iron Mountain

© 2015 Francesca Quarto

Burton, MI 48509

Cover design by Clarissa Yeo

Printed in United States of America

Printed by

Tell-Tale Publishing Group, LLC
5174 Peri Street
Swartz Creek, MI 48473
www.tell-talepublishing.com

Thistle Imprint

THISTLE

Dedication

Because life is a mixture of all kinds of magic, one can dream and love, discover and grow, all of this with the help of others. This book is dedicated to some of those uniquely wonderful people. My husband, Patrick, who helped me to dream and loved me in my quest. Virginia and Michael, who kept it alive with their belief in me. And my patient and insightful editor, Elizabeth Fortin-Hinds, who challenged me to reach a little deeper and find more Magic in myself.

Chapter 1

The sleeping town of Iron Mountain was not in its first yawn of awakening when I stepped foot on its deserted main street. The clouds streaking across the face of the moon obscured much of its pale light. It had taken me twenty-five minutes of heavy trudging through the snow to arrive at this tableau of stores, brooding and silent in the dark. Only the old fashioned street lights shed any warmth on the scene. I gazed around me as my breath billowed out, adding to the fog that clung to the cold ground like a spectral throw rug. I tried to peer into the closed store fronts as I passed, but the lack of light kept their interiors a secret for later discovery.

I straightened up and made a slow semi-circle, studying the mist-shrouded mountains surrounding me like some crouching beasts in the grey light before dawn. It was sadly quiet, like a bell without a clapper. I felt a chill not related to the cold. I looked over my shoulder for the umpteenth time. Nothing. I turned back. Still, there was something off. *Geez*! I thought, looking back yet again. Still nothing. *Totally paranoid, that's what I am.* There was a strange smell riding the waves of cold air, stirring as I moved on.

My senses were on high alert as they always were when I was in an unfamiliar environment. I might be overly cautious, but I was still alive and as my mom says in her understated way, "Life is a careful process, Cathleen, my pet. So watch where you place your feet." In her slow Irish brogue, it had always sounded more ominous somehow.

Actually, it was mom who convinced me to make this odyssey. I had come to a major cross-roads in my career and life and had to make some serious decisions. Mom knew I needed the mountains and forests to find the peace and freedom I'd lost living in a big city. I'd complained to her many times that the only thing natural about the metropolis of Pittsburgh was the ubiquitous pigeons! And the men I'd met weren't even as bright as the birds.

The snow crunching under my heavy boots penetrated the frigid air like the sound of muted firecrackers as I made a path into the heart of this Appalachian town. A village really, with so many artifacts from the 1800s, I felt like I'd stepped through a time portal. The weight of its long history bore down on me like the gaze of a hungry raptor. *Did I make a huge mistake coming here?* I speculated as my thoughts drifted along with the heavy snow.

Like so much in life, surprises and unforeseen circumstances are more common than flies in summer. I came into an unexpected inheritance when my grandfather passed away last year in Ireland shortly after my last visit with him. We always had a special relationship that brought us together in laughter at the wonderful stories of his youth on his beautiful Emerald Isle.

I had no idea that my grandfather was rich... let alone extremely rich. He had lived quite modestly. Overnight, I became a wealthy young woman, which helped support my already independent nature. Simultaneously, I also became the stand-alone O'Brien from my granddad's side of that far-flung clan.

By contrast, my grandfather's youngest son, Liam, my father, hadn't left a dime to his family when he died, five years before my granddad. When he was lost under the swift current of the Alleghany River my dad was working as part of a crew on a local fishing boat. That was one of his "pick-up" jobs as my mom often described Dad's occasional work. Soon after his disappearance, my mother moved back to her beloved Ireland. I managed to sell our small house and property for her, so she could live comfortably in her childhood home of County Kirk.

I stayed behind to finish college with the help of scholarships and grants. By the time I obtained my Master's degree, I had become a competent "barista" at a local coffee house and had accumulated lots of dreams but little money. That's about the time I began to take inventory of my life and resources.

Though dad didn't have much of material value, he did leave me two unique gifts; a wealth of remembered Irish folklore wrapped inside his lovely Irish brogue and, oh, yes... a penchant for Gaelic Magic.

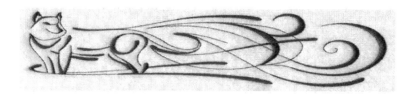

Chapter 2

My father was a Celtic Mage, a wizard, by any other name, a practitioner of Magic.

He was versed in the secret arts of the ancient mystics and the healing powers of the *Green Mother*. His father and his father's father back to medieval times were *all* schooled by this method, handing down knowledge of the arcane magic of the Gaelic Druids and other myth-bound cults, over the centuries.

These secretive keepers of the old ways were sheltered and protected from the rampant persecution of their kind by the small village of my father's ancestors for untold generations. They repaid this debt to the people of the village by defending them from practitioners of the black arts and the evil witches that stalked the land and the innocent, in those darkest of times.

As he was trained, my father taught me, his only child, tales of the whispering heather on that far away Isle. We would huddle together in our secret forest places, practicing chants and charms and magic wards for hours, sometimes well into the new day. As a small girl, I would often fall asleep in some dimly lit cave, curled up at my father's feet while his chanting voice swirled around me like a cape, settling over me in cozy, secure warmth. Without realizing it, I was learning to tap into and control the power of the earth and the elements of nature, and use this pure energy of the *Green Mother* to protect myself. No cherished stories of Leprechauns for me. My tales were of monsters and demons that roamed our world and my lullabies were the soft chants of magic words to ward myself against these dark forces. I was taught in total secrecy and only mother knew of my apprenticeship into the Guild of the Green Wizards.

I swore a sacred oath when I was old enough to pronounce the words, to protect the natural realm against any Dark Magic. Just as our clan had sheltered that small village during the blackest days of earth, the O'Briens, including me, would continue their vigilance against evil forces, wherever they threatened this fragile, mortal life. Because I was pledged to the *Green Mother* my life was filled with wondrous feats of magic and as I progressed in my training, I realized that my father, Liam, was my very own Merlin.

Father told me many times about a recurring dream he'd had since I was "a wee bere" as he called me, in which he saw me dressed as a Celtic warrior. He claimed that my Magic would prove strong and baffle my enemies in days to come. At the time, I deemed this "enemy" to be Margaret O'Malley, my fourth grade nemesis. Little did I know as I walked the quiet streets of Iron Mountain, that my very life would depend upon the Celtic chants and ancient spells I repeated back to him, as we wandered together around the foothills of the towering Alleghany Mountains.

I stayed in Pittsburgh for several months after I received my inheritance. I couldn't wrap my head around the concept of being wealthy. Also, I felt obligated to fulfill my two-year contract at the radio station where I worked. I sometimes wonder why. At first I had thought my Masters degree in communications was the primary reason for getting hired. Then I realized there probably hadn't been much competition as my on-air slot wasn't exactly career building. I was hired to host a call in talk show airing in the darkest hours of the night, called *Night Crawlers*. Pretty aptly named considering some of the bottom feeders and creeps I had to listen to. Mostly, they called in ranting about body snatchers, alien invasions, or exorcisms gone wrong. For some reason, after a particularly annoying show, I decided to make some changes. To start, I followed my heart. I purchased my own radio station, changing the environment of my life and future. Iron Mountain was as different from the grit of a big city as a mud puddle is from the Atlantic.

At twenty-four, I was considered reasonably attractive, if somewhat a loner, but my new life's vision now reflected a trained Celtic Wizard and the newly minted owner and General Manager of WHIP Radio the on-air voice of Iron Mountain, in the heart of the Appalachian Mountains.

With all the insecurities of a young person striking out alone into the world, I began to question my new position in life and my ability to make a success of it. Then I thought about the guy I bought the station from, Malcom Prescott. *Maybe I'm still young, but I'm a darn sight smarter than the previous owner.* He had sarcastically told me the call letters "WHIP" signified how the station always "whipped" their competition. *Yeah, right. That's why he had to sell at a loss to me.* Of course it could have had something to do with that harassment suit against their old sales manager.

That's how I discovered this little gem of electronic media in the deep woods of Appalachia. There was an article in a media journal about its impending sale, due to what Malcom Prescott called the legal costs of defending himself against unfounded and liable allegations.

Translated, it seemed the ex-sales manager, a sleazy ex-high school jock who still wore his letter sweater to local high school games was trying to impress his secretary with his self-imagined charms. I had fired him and kept the secretary.

As I came to the end of the block, I crossed over to check out the only light I saw in an otherwise bleak and shadowy town. As I approached, I realized Iron Mountain had a bakery. I was happy to find the nasty smell that had shadowed my progress , disappeared under the yeasty fragrance of fresh breads, doughnuts, and sweet rolls that seemed to cling to the fog and rise up to entice me as I crunched along. I couldn't help smiling at the homey feeling that came over me. Thrusting my hands deeper into the pockets of my heavy coat, I walked faster, with purpose now, toward the yellow glow painting the snow and dispelling the shadows.

My lonesome journey through a strange place ended the minute I stepped over the threshold into a fragrant oasis. A voice called out in a rich, deep baritone "Welcome to The Ugly Baker's Sweets and Treats. What pray tell are you doing up this early in the morning young lady? And what brings you to our snowy mountain paradise?"

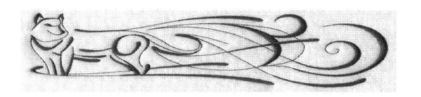

Chapter 3

I stood with my mouth hanging like a door off its hinges and openly stared at the very short man addressing me from his perch on a three-legged stool. Catching my breath after my long trudge through several feet of snow I stammered, "Forgive my barging in on you. I was just out looking the town over when I saw your light. The only one on, actually," I said, removing my knit hat to shake off the snow. Released, my thick auburn hair did its version of curly locks on steroids.

While I was trying to bring some kind of order to my unruly mane, the baker said, "Well, it *is* only four in the morning, so most folks are still snug in their beds. But I don't keep banker's hours as you can see." The little man was smiling broadly as he climbed down from his stool.

He couldn't have been more than 4 feet tall, yet he radiated such energy and charm that I took an instant liking to him. His bearded face and arms wore a dusting of flour and his bald head gleamed with a soft sheen of perspiration, reflecting the glow from the over-head lights. He looked very strong despite his small stature and I was admiring his biceps when he thrust a freshly baked croissant under my nose.

"Better try one before they disappear into the mouths of the locals." I hadn't even registered that he'd moved! He smiled at me as I made all the appropriate yummy sounds and then began busying himself with baking the ready loaves.

He called back to me from a gaping oven, "We don't get too many tourists, so I guess you just moved here. Am I right?"

"Yes," I answered through the buttery flakes of glory. "Moved here from Pittsburgh a few days ago and wanted to investigate my new hometown." This sounded strange to me, calling Iron Mountain my new hometown. I had barely unpacked my tooth brush and was already scouting out the natives. It was due to my innate curiosity, not some desire to start digging a hole for my roots, or at least that's what I told myself.

"My name's Gus Flores, by the way," he said, coming over to where I carefully leaned against a sparkling white wall covered in antique looking rolling pins, cookie cutters and other vintage baking paraphernalia. He caught me as I licked the last sweet morsel off my fingers and flashed a quick smile.

"Probably the only Hispanic dwarf you'll ever meet," he said, laughing. I found his deep voice complimented his general appearance as it was warm and mellow.

"I'm Cathleen O'Brien, the last of my clan that you'll ever meet," I responded and offered him my unlicked hand with a broad smile. He wiped his hand clean of flour on the apron tied securely around his waist and took mine into what was a surprisingly strong grip .I was surprised again at the strength this small man radiated as I smiled down at him. He'd made me feel genuinely welcomed and I knew I'd be establishing a happy morning routine coming into his cheery bakery before work.

"Why don't you sit for a spell, Cathleen?" he asked warmly.

"Thanks, it is pretty nippy out there," I said, happy for the offer to warm myself up before my trek over to the radio station.

Taking the small cushioned chair he nodded to near the cash register. I looked over at him and said "I was wondering about your shop's peculiar name."

"Well, little lady, just take a look at me and tell me it isn't appropriate!" He had a smile on his face, but there was a hint of sadness in his eyes. "I know folks around here think I'm a great baker, but that doesn't change the fact that they still look at me as a strange, weird, ugly little guy. Hence, "The Ugly Baker".

I didn't know what to say, but then my unfiltered response mechanism kicked in and I blurted out, "I think some people around here obviously don't appreciate the little gem they have in you." He was laughing when I realized my phrase, "little gem" was not going to be an award winning argument on his behalf. *I can be so lame at times* I thought to myself after I dribbled out a weak "sorry" comment which he quickly waived off as he kept chuckling.

His bread was about finished and so fragrant my mouth started watering. I wanted to know about my new home so Gus took a break and began giving me some background. "I can give you a quick history lesson if you'd like," he said, while automatically dusting powdered sugar over some newly minted donuts.

"The town of Iron Mountain was founded around 1814, or so the local historian, Talbot Frazer says. It was a thriving place at one time, with the region's most productive coal mine. It made certain folk millionaires and others it turned into coughing, wheezing, sickly, young men. If the mine didn't kill them with its constant tunnel collapses, the black dust they sucked in eventually did. But they kept going back under the ground because the work was steady and the coal mine owners literally owned *them* too. They provided the shacks they lived in and owned the company store where they bought the food for their families at exorbitant prices. Things sure don't change much in this world do they little lady?" He grew quiet for a moment and I asked if he'd been born here.

"I moved to Iron Mountain over 30 years ago, just passing through as I was hiking the Appalachian Trail," he answered.

"You hiked that trail!" I said a bit too loudly.

"Well, yes I did" he answered with a wry grin on his face.

"That's an adventure I've thought of taking from time to time," I said.

He was putting his freshly baked goods into their display cases when he looked back at me and asked, "So why haven't you done it?"

"Just kind of unsure about doing it alone I guess. Between the mountain lions, bears, snakes, and other things that might find me a tempting dinner, I just haven't worked up the courage."

"Guess I just looked like a snack to them," Gus was chuckling "not really worth the effort to catch me. Besides, I can climb a tree pretty darn quick when necessary!"

I was asking more about the town when the front door banged open, trailed by a gust of cold wind and snow as a very tall, uniformed man stepped into the cozy shop. As he stamped his feet like he was putting out fires, the cold radiated from his clothes, and I felt the chill from my perch nearby. He smiled broadly and said, "Morning, Gus!"

"Good morning, Sheriff Tate. Meet Cathleen O'Brien," he nodded over in my direction "late of Pittsburg, PA and newly moved to our fair town. Cathleen, this is Jason Tate our town constable".

"Nice to meet you, Miss O'Brien," he said, turning to me in my snug corner. "Welcome to the Appalachian Way. How are you and your family finding our little burrow in the snow?"

I managed to smile, but my voice was choked by the large lump in my throat. I stared at his handsome, rugged face and became helplessly fixated on the black patch that covered his left eye.

When I was finally able to speak I covered my awkward silence saying in a small voice, "I'm liking it more and more, Sheriff." I was grinning like a young girl who just discovered the boy she liked in school thought she wasn't a nerd after all. When he smiled back I knew I wanted to see more of that sly grin in days to come. "I actually don't have any family living with me, Sheriff Tate. Just me and my dog Ollie," I said,

"Oh?" he said, giving me a rather searching look that immediately brought on a blush. I squirmed, hoping he'd think it was just the cold coloring my cheeks. I noticed he seemed rather pleased with that particular information. "Just call me Jason," he said to me. I heard a distinct chuckle come from the display cases and figured Gus was enjoying this ancient verbal dance between man and woman.

The Sheriff's hair was mostly hidden under a brown knit cap with the emblem "IMS D" stitched across the front, but what I could see of it was very black and thick. Even with only one eye, this sheriff seemed to see everything and that included my nervous response to him. "So, where's Ollie?" he asked while removing his heavy leather gloves. "Hope you didn't leave him outside in this cold weather."

"He's back in Pittsburgh with my girlfriend. He'll be joining me in a few weeks. I wanted to get settled before I introduced him to his new home."

He smiled warmly and I knew he loved dogs just by the way he said, "Ollie will have lots of running room up here."

"I'm looking forward to having him with me again and we *both* enjoy running," I responded, trying my best to look fit and up to the physical challenge of the mountain roads.

"Well," he said, smiling sweetly, like he knew I was overstating my abilities just a tad. "I really love running myself. Maybe we can run together one day when the weather is nice again."

I smiled weakly at this prospect and said "Sounds like an invitation Ollie and I can't refuse. Of course, from what I've seen of the weather so far, that will be sometime in June!

He laughed, then shaking his head in agreement and looking more serious said, "If I may ask, Miss O'Brien, how'd you come to move here from the big city?"

"Please, Cathleen is fine." I said, as I looked up at his handsome face I noticed he had a strong jawline with a small dimple in his chin. "I bought your radio station, WHIP, and will be its General Manager" I replied, trying to tap down the little bit of pride that crept into my voice. He looked more closely at me and I felt myself blush at the attention.

"So, *you're* the new owner. We were all wondering what to expect and frankly, you weren't it!" I bristled a bit at that remark, but he quickly smoothed my feathers by saying, "Actually, I believe you'll be a very welcome change at WHIP Radio. They needed fresh blood down there and certainly someone with more intelligence than a duck!"

We all laughed at that and I replied, "I can't speak to a duck's IQ, but I can state firmly that I will try to exceed it! By the way, where exactly is the station from here?"

Gus looked up at me from the donut case and answered, "It's just down the street a ways. If you leave here and turn right, you can't miss it."

I thanked him and decided I'd answered enough questions. "I'd best be going, Gus, but I want to thank you so much for your hospitality. I'll be back for some of your wonderful goodies. Nice meeting you, Sheriff Tate. Jason." I was out the door before they could see my knees knock when the good looking lawman shook my hand again, holding it a breath too long while looking intently into my eyes. I felt a little shudder that had nothing to do with the storm blowing outside.

I was stuffing my hair under my now damp knit hat, when I looked back quickly through the glass on the door and saw the town Sheriff staring after me. That put a smile on my face and a bit more enthusiasm in my step as I began my slog toward my very own radio station.

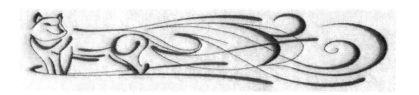

Chapter 4

I decided to put off my visit until the afternoon after spotting what appeared to be a few stray dogs hanging around the back of the closed station. From a distance, they seemed very big and looked decidedly unfriendly, as they were obviously squabbling over some bit of food. I could hear their intimidating growls clearly, in the crisp winter air. Whatever they had was clamped between two sets of jaws in a tug of war and I didn't want to meet the loser!

Guess small mountain towns don't believe in leash ordinances, I thought as I retreated quickly and I hoped, unnoticed, back the way I'd come.

My house was still the only structure I could pick out in the murkiness of pre-dawn. This was because I'd left every light on so I could use them like a homing beacon to find my way home. I'm not sure what I would have done if my neighbors had to get up at the ungodly hour I normally did.

I was thinking about my old "Night Crawlers" show as I walked at a brisk pace, my boots making what seemed an unnaturally loud commotion on the crusty snow. Thinking about how I would run my newly acquired radio station, I suddenly began to feel twitchy and a definite vibration of fear ran down my back. I slowed down to listen. There it was again. I heard a definite crunching of snow as someone, or something was coming up behind me.

I spun around in time to see a flash of black in the feeble light coming from my distant windows and felt myself being driven to the ground. The breath was knocked out of me and the only yell for help I could make sounded like a violin being tortured by a seven year old. My hands were instinctively doing that grappling thing that drowning people do when they are being rescued and I found myself grabbing fists full of thick fur. *The dogs! I must have smelled like the croissant*, I thought, knowing immediately that was ridiculous! They had followed me and now three of them circled like a demented merry-go-round full of salivating, snarling creatures watching me fight with what was probably their leader. I watched this trio closing in to where I lay under the massive weight of the humongous black dog. Its hot breath reeked with the pungent smell of rotten meat and the saliva dripping off its gaping jaws was dangerously close to falling into my own open mouth. I quickly stopped calling for help to avoid that unpleasantness and concentrated on his eyes. They had the look of dried blood. A deep, lifeless red.

I might be considered on the small side at 5 feet 4 inches and 120 pounds, but I focused all of my strength into my arms to keep the snarling dog away from my face and neck. My father had taught me how to gather my strength from my core of Magic, but only in drastic situations as it would leave me exhausted and vulnerable in the end. This was definitely a life and death situation as his teeth seemed longer and closer by the second. I gasped out the ancient words for strengthening of body "*brutha oscadh*" and lifted the ferocious beast off my chest. He looked as surprised as I did when it worked and his upper body was dangling a foot above my grimacing face.

When I could breathe more normally, I started yelling for help. Almost immediately I heard a car door slamming and running feet crunching across the snow. The dog heard my would-be rescuer too. Before he could get in a nibble, he was off me and hidden in the shadows along with his mangy pals, who must have run off at the sound of the vehicle.

"Are you ok?" It was the good looking Sheriff. He took my arm and got me to my feet while I scanned the darkest patches of trees around us for the marauding canines. I looked down at my hands and there were several clumps of black fur poking out between my gloved fingers.

"What the heck *was* that?" I asked, my voice trembling with the residual fear of the encounter and the exhaustion that was now creeping into my limbs. I could smell the rotten scent of the creature's body as I tried to brush snow off my coat and jeans.

Jason must have smelled it too because he said, "You're going to want to get your coat cleaned, Cathleen. You don't want Ollie to hide from you when you bring him home."

I tried to smile, but it slipped from my face and I asked again, "Jason, seriously…what was that creature ?"

"I only got a brief look, but it could have been a young timber wolf," he replied. "Let's get you inside and make sure you weren't injured, Cathleen."

We crossed into the bright pool of light spilling from my front room window. My house only lacked a neon sign reading, "Home Sweet Home," to complete the feeling of comfort and safety I felt. Of course, the Sheriff's strong arm around my waist didn't hurt either.

"Wow! I guess that's what I can expect when I venture outdoors at four in the morning," I said, trying to sound much less upset than I felt. I was rubbing my arms which still felt pumped with adrenaline after fending off my mangy attacker.

"Trust me," Jason said, "that was pretty unusual for these parts. Wolves don't make it down from the mountains except when prey is scarce up there."

"So why today? Why here?" I asked after checking out my clothing and determining there were no puncture marks anywhere. I pushed open the front door and gestured for the

Sheriff to follow as I wandered through a maze of boxes into the kitchen and plugged in the coffee pot hoping for a shot of energy from the caffeine. My legs were still shaking from the after-shock of my encounter, but I managed to look over at Jason like I was in control of the situation. I wished I could go into the woods behind my house to wrap my vibrating arms around the nearest tree. I needed to ask the *Mother* to help recharge my magical energies. Meanwhile, fussing around my kitchen seemed to help and having Jason's undivided attention was definitely giving me a boost…at least an ego boost.

Jason stood near the kitchen table and watching me prepare the coffee finally answered my questions.

"Hard to hazard a guess about those critters, Cathleen, but I'd say they were young wolves somehow separated from their pack, maybe kicked out by some of the adults and started a new pack. The big one that had you pinned down was likely the new pack's leader, the "alpha". They might have been trying to establish new hunting grounds around here and your place was unfortunately part of it."

"You seem pretty conversant on the subject of wolves, Jason," I commented as I turned away from him for a minute and filled the pot with tap water. When I looked back at him, he looked at me rather closely and answered, "Not really. Just picked up a few things here and there from Gus I think."

"Are you and Gus pretty close?" I asked.

"He's really been more like a Dad to me over the years, so yeah. He's a good man and something of an authority when it comes to the wildlife in these parts. So I guess he taught me quite a bit."

I wondered why his own father wasn't a part of the conversation, but didn't probe into what might be sensitive places. I was lucky to have such a close relationship with my own father, but then not too many girls could go to their dads for the best spell to cast on a wood troll.

By now the coffee was brewed to a tantalizing aroma of perfection and as I looked into several boxes to unearth two mugs. Jason made himself at home and opened my fridge, taking out the only item stored there, the cream. "I do love my cream," I said, rather embarrassed by my lack of provisions. His smile at that comment warmed me up so much I didn't think I'd need the coffee. *Why is this guy having such an effect on my normally friendly, but at a distance, kind of attitude?* I was looking forward to solving that particular mystery very much.

"I do my coffee black and strong. Don't like to complicate matters," he said with a chuckle before he nearly drained the mug I had just poured.

Must have been cold and thirsty I smiled to myself. Moving back into the box-littered living room I said, "I'd invite you to sit, but I can't find my furniture."

He chuckled. "No problem, I really have to be going anyway." He put his mug on top of my mom's old piano and went to the door. Looking down at me when I'd thanked him once more for his timely rescue, he said, "Best keep off the streets if it's dark and you are alone, Cathleen, and you might want to stay out of the wooded areas around here too, just to be on the safe side."

"But that's why I moved here, Jason, to get closer to nature, not to hide from it."

His one green eye looked back at me intently as he replied, "Lots of things hide around here. Some hide for safety and some for fear. There's no shame in either. Have a good day, Cathleen. Hope to see you around town."

It took a while before it dawned on me that he had to have been following me at a distance to have arrived at the precise moment I needed him most. *A coincidence* I thought? I never believed in it. My time on that whacky call-in show taught me a few things about scary too.

Like my father used to say "a coincidence is only a rubber band that's stretched to its limit." I never really figured out what he meant exactly, but I knew I didn't want to be around when the rubber band snapped.

Chapter 5

The run in with the wild dogs, or wolves as Jason suspected, had pretty much drained me and the coffee hadn't really helped much. I found my unmade bed after Jason had gone and after taking a few minutes to turn out enough wattage to light the town.

My watch said nine-thirty. *Geese, I've lost most of the day*! I thought as I got out from under my quilt and dad's old woolen army blanket from when he served with the Irish Armed forces as a very young man. He was great at commandeering items while he was in. A regular Irish Houdini, he was also able to get out of any trouble. His charms were legendary in the family. My mom always said he wasn't born with the luck of the Irish, he stole it!

After a long shower to comfort the bruising I discovered on my back and arms, I put on my going to town face and dressed in mountain-girl style. My boots and layering of two warm sweaters would definitely be needed as it had snowed heavily during my long nap. I kept thinking back to my scary encounter as I finished packing on enough clothes for two more people. *Guess a little puppy after Ollie passes on is out of the question,* I mused. Ollie was a senior citizen and would likely have only a few more years as my companion. A cat would probably disappear into the den of a wily coyote. That left fish or a bird as possible future companions in my rustic mountain home. Nope. No good at Frisbee or cuddling.

Since I had no food in the fridge besides the cream and some assorted power bars I'd found crumbling in my back pack, I cranked the heat up to a welcome back smoldering seventy degrees. Bundled up like an Eskimo, I ventured down the short but empty road into town. I felt more secure in the daylight, but still kept a guarded watch at the fringes of the woods surrounding me, searching for any kind of toothy snout poking out in my general direction. I knew the first stop would be at The Ugly Baker's. I needed coffee and company.

Gus was busy with a shop full of customers. Some were lounging over fragrant, steaming cups of coffee or hot chocolate, leaning on counters, or up against the bakery's festooned walls. Others waited patiently in line, talking in a low hum about the weather. Even with all this distraction, Gus still managed to wave and smile in my direction. He had an assistant it seemed, but I wasn't clear on their relationship as they kept up a steady stream of rather humorous banter that everyone pretty much ignored. I assumed this was a traditional entertainment around there. "I've grown an inch since I asked you to bring me that tray of glazed!" Gus hollered at the helper who'd just ducked back into the shop's spacious pantry.

I finally worked my way to the front of the shuffling line and after another greeting, ordered a large coffee, heavy on the cream and a cake donut with cinnamon. When Gus handed over a huge cup and my favorite sugar jolt, he motioned me closer to the counter. He was perched on a sort of rolling stairway that he was able to move from place to place as needed and was now sitting on the top stair. "I hear you had a run in with some local canines, Cathleen."

"Wow!" I said. "It doesn't take long for happenings to get to your attention, does it Gus?"

He demurred at what he seemed to take as a compliment, though I was not feeling too happy that my encounter with the "Hound of the Baskervilles" had become gossip fodder for the locals. I must have transmitted some "big city girl" attitude regarding privacy issues as Gus was quickly telling me that only he and Jason knew of my adventure.

"We should have warned you not to stray off the beaten path, Cathleen," he said with real concern in his voice..

"But I wasn't *off* the road, Gus. I just followed your directions and went over to the station where the dogs, or wolves, or whatever must have spotted me. I started right back toward my house when I was jumped, literally!"

Gus seemed almost distraught with my comments and was about to say more, but a new customer was behind me making conversation with no one in particular about what kind of treat to buy. Gus noticed him and said, "Mornin', Joe," by way of acknowledging his position in line.

"Catch you later, Cathleen. Have a great day," he said in a cheerful voice. Then he added after a second, "And stay safe."

"Sure, Gus. You have a good one too." I answered as I exited the shop, clutching my treat and hot coffee close to my bulky coat.

I was in the middle of my boxes a few hours later when I heard a knock on the door and then saw Jason's face peering in the front window. *Glad I wasn't unpacking in my underwear!* I thought as I rushed to extricate myself from the newspapers and boxes strewn around me. "Hey Jason, what a nice surprise!" I said as if I meant it, because I did. "Are you looking for the night prowler or just checking up on my whereabouts?"

He smiled that crooked, enigmatic smile I liked the first time we met. Was it really only in the wee hours this morning? "I see you're hard at work still looking for your furniture," he said stepping over a pile of broken-down boxes. Mess or no mess, Jason had a relaxed air and very comfortable way about himself. "Looks like you've made some progress, Cathleen. Been living off your coffee and cream I suppose." He added the last comment with a teasing smirk on his face.

"I was out earlier for coffee and one of Gus's wonderful donuts and decided this was more important than grocery shopping. For the moment at least," I said as I was trying to stuff paper wrappings into the ever-growing pile of recyclable trash bags.

After moving the giant stuffed Panda bear I've dragged around with me since I was three, Jason perched himself on the piano stool. "By the way, Cathleen, how are you getting around? I didn't see a car in your garage."

I took a minute to realize he must have looked into my garage window to know that particular detail. "Well, Sheriff Tate, you've obviously been snooping around my property. Care to tell me why?" I didn't ask this in a snide way, but still demanding and he could see I wasn't happy to have that kind of surveillance.

"Sorry, Cathleen," he said and, somehow, he managed to look like the offended one.

Geeze, I'm the one with the nosey cop looking into my windows!

"I was only checking to make certain you didn't have any unwanted visitor."

"My garage seems an unlikely place for one doesn't it?" I replied a bit more tartly (sort of a McIntosh response rather than a Red Delicious).

He stood up and came over to where I was standing. Looking down from his 6 foot something, he said softly, "O.K. The truth is I wanted to ask you to breakfast, but my vehicle is in the shop, so I thought we could take yours. Gus loaned me his pick-up so I could come out here. Sorry, I guess I wanted to make a better impression on you than I just did."

I felt the blush start in my toes and work its way up to my cheeks. "No," I said looking down, embarrassed. "I'm sorry, Jason, for being so short with you. I think I'm still a little unnerved by that attack on me. And I'd love to escape all this," I said, shrugging my head toward the unpacking of my old life.

"Does your offer still stand?" I asked, with a look that I hoped was contrite and sweeter than my last harsh words.

His crooked grin was back in place. "Well, since my patrol car is out of commission for a few more hours, give me thirty minutes to round up my Deputy's car and get back here."

He seemed so genuinely pleased that I laughed and said "I'll use that time to make myself more presentable for my new neighbors."

Turning back to me as he stepped back out into the cold he said "Don't change anything on my account. I think you look pretty terrific in sweats and flannel!"

As I locked the door behind him, I caught a reflection of myself in the hall mirror; "Not too shabby if I do say so myself!"

Chapter 6

He took us to the *Sun and Moon Restaurant,* a very oriental name for what turned out to be as decidedly American as *Sesame Street.* "I take it this place is only open for breakfast and dinner," I ventured.

"It's our only restaurant outside of Baker's Diner and the owner feels she deserves the afternoon off after serving breakfast from 6 to11:30," he said. "And I don't think you'll get any better food anywhere."

He sure seemed anxious to please me so I guessed my earlier crankiness was forgiven. Our drive to the restaurant took more than twenty-five minutes and I figured I'd better start looking for a car ASAP. Mine was driven into the hard ground of Pittsburgh. As my eyes passed over the unfamiliar scenery, I thought back to my move here. Jason didn't seem to mind my dreamy silence as I sat quietly watching and remembering as the snowy landscape slid by.

I had taken the only cab from the Appalachian Regional Airport when I arrived in Iron Mountain on my way to my new home. I'd been relieved to see it had an actual control tower and we weren't landing by landmarks alone. The trip from there to my new house took another 45 minutes. We must have impressed the locals we passed, as I caught a few curtains being tweaked open for a peek, as we drove like a slow funeral procession of one, along the snowy back roads. Taxis weren't a common sight in these deep-wooded areas I imagined.

I used my inner sight to scan the nearby woods. I had a persistent feeling that something was watching our progress, something that didn't belong in this pristine mountain setting. My intuition told me that I was right, but I was unable to determine who, or what, raised my magic hackles, so I turned my attention to the more pleasant task of studying Jason's profile. His nose was straight, except for a small dent in the middle of the bridge, perhaps from a rowdy criminal. I couldn't help wondering if that was how he came by the eye patch as well. He glanced my way, and I quickly looked ahead at the snow-pelted windshield.

We'd passed a car dealership on the way to the restaurant and I tried to cover my staring by saying, "do you think they have any Jeeps at that dealership back there?"

"Morgan King is the owner, and a really honest guy, especially for a car dealer, Cathleen," he replied with a chuckle. "Actually, we've been good friends since we were kids. I'm sure he'd do right by you. What kind of Jeep are you looking for?"

I thought for a minute and then blurted out, "A red Wrangler". It felt right saying it and I knew that would be the car I'd love--sporty and good on these slippery roads, too.

"Well, that's pretty specific," he said with a smile. "I don't know if you can find a red one, but I know he has a few Jeeps on his lot. If you'd like I can take you over there after breakfast."

"Great."

We arrived just before they stopped serving breakfast and both ordered the *Lumber Jack* with enough food for a small village, served on brightly colored mismatched dishes. While we ate from the bounty spread before us, Jason asked lots of questions about my life and background. After a while I felt like I was being interviewed and said smiling "Hey! When do I get to interrogate you, Sheriff?"

"Well, guess as the lawman here, I'm used to being the one asking. Sorry about that," he said, grinning sheepishly. "You're right. Fire away."

"Were you born around here?"

"I've been here my entire life," he answered, "but I did leave for college and after graduating, to work overseas for a short time."

"Army? Navy?" He looked away for a blink and then said, "No, just a few out-of-country assignments for a private security. My Masters degree is in Criminal Law so it seemed a good fit.

"Were you in law enforcement then?" I asked after a big sip from my bright blue mug.

"Actually, I was. I headed up a unit guarding some facilities owned by a large corporate entity."

"That sounds exciting," I said, smiling, and tried to imagine this macho guy running around in a turban and robe like Laurence of Arabia, guarding oil fields for some Sheik.

As we kept talking, I was impressed by what seemed to be genuine humility from this very accomplished man. He never bragged about his achievements, though at one point said quietly that he was the youngest Sheriff ever to hold that post in Iron Mountain, or any of the surrounding towns. Talking with him felt refreshing after I had worked with so many men with super egos. The world of media I left behind in Pittsburgh was populated with game players and users, trying to get a spot as an on-air celebrity. I never had much competition for my spot though. My radio persona was more attractive to the *Night of the Living Dead* types and aired in the wee hours of the morning when mostly weirdoes and insomniacs were awake...and me of course.

After finding out he had no living family and was in law enforcement because he wanted to see justice done, I let him get in another question.

"Why'd you buy WHIP Radio, Cathleen, if you don't mind my asking?" I took a deep breath and decided I could tell him my story without fear of being judged as some kind of opportunist taking advantage of a backwoods community. "After I finished my Masters in Communications, I was lucky enough to land a job with a popular Pittsburgh radio station," I said. "I had my own call-in talk show. That's when I found out two life-altering things; radio can be just as full of garbage and glory as TV and that I loved being a part of that."

"What kind of show did you have?" he asked.

"My show was called "Night Crawlers," if that tells you anything."

He laughed, "Like the worms we fish with."

"Yeah, and some of my callers could scare the scales off a barracuda," I said grimly. "I had to hire a personal body guard to escort me home after I signed off air, because of all the threats to end my rule as *Queen of the Night Crawlers*. That was what one persistent weirdo dubbed me anyway." Although I laughed, a chill went through me like a brain freeze and I rubbed my arms. "I can't believe I'm still a little rattled by that attack. Guess I might want to think about hiring another body guard."

Leaning across the table, Jason placed a large, well-callused hand over mine and looking deeply into my eyes and said, "I plan to ensure that no harm will come to you in Iron Mountain, Cathleen. I'm watching out for you." Within a heartbeat, I'd gone from feeling anxious about this new life of mine to feeling that it was the best thing I had ever done for myself. Looking back at this interesting, intelligent and somewhat mysterious man, I also knew he was a big part of why. And it didn't hurt that he was so handsome in his mountain gear that I felt like yodeling when he smiled at me!

His eye was a deep green, like the forests around us. We both smiled, and I wish I knew him well enough to ask about his eye.

As if he had noticed me looking at his eye patch, he leaned back against his seat and said, "You've showed great restraint. Aren't you going to ask the million dollar question?"

"No. I figured if you wanted me to know, you'd tell me."

He nodded, slowly, as if pleasantly surprised with my respect for his privacy. Then, he shyly recounted how, on a fishing trip with his buddy when he was about 14, his friend had been showing off his casting skills when he tried for a long fly cast and caught Jason in his left eye with the hook. "Luckily, it never affected my shooting ability, since no matter how many times they told me to stop closing one eye when I aimed, I didn't listen," he said, chuckling. "And I think it actually improved my observation skills. This pirate tribute," he explained, touching his patch, "is here to keep young children from screaming in terror while a new and hopefully more comfortable artificial eye is being completed. Unfortunately, there's no guarantee I can wear one because of the way the accident disfigured the socket. Oh boy," he stopped himself. "I'm sorry to go on about such an unpleasant topic."

"You're fine," I said. "Thanks for your candor, and your trust."

His only response was to shrug his shoulders and hold my steady gaze. I felt I had just made a stronger connection with him than some guys I'd dated for months. I admired his ability to joke about his injury, and his sensitivity to my reaction. I realized there were a growing number of things I admired about him and hoped he felt the same about me. *Hm, this could get interesting,* I thought, still smiling at this modern-day mountain man.

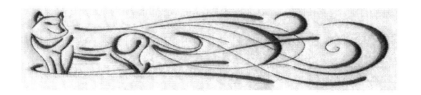

Chapter 7

After an hour of very pleasant conversation and a mountaineer-size breakfast, I soon found myself standing in Morgan King's pale blue office. It looked strangely like a dentist's digs with lots of stainless steel furnishings and four-year-old magazines. "It's a pleasure to finally meet the new owner of our radio station," he was saying, as he squeezed my hand into something akin to crippling carpel tunnel. He was a veritable leviathan of a man, at least three-hundred-and-fifty pounds and probably six-foot-five, probably more. But for all that weight, he looked very muscular and moved with the grace of a cat in his size 16 plus shoes.

Must be a body builder, I mused. "It's nice to meet you, Mr. King."

"Please," he said, "just call me Morgan. All the folks do."

Before he released my now almost numb hand, I felt a peculiar vibration run through my arm and down my side. I gave an internal shrug and checked it off to sleep deprivation or post wolf attack nerves. "Thanks, Morgan. I'd like to see some of the Jeeps you have in stock if that could be arranged," I said with as much authority as I could muster, wanting to establish my car-buying credentials quickly.

"Well, Cathleen, or do you prefer Miss O'Brien?" he asked, while he was flashing me a toothy salesman smile. His eyes seemed to be taking my measure, calculating just how far his smooth lines would take him.

"Cathleen is fine," I replied with my own show of toothy charm.

"Great," he said, then let's just stroll out to the back lot and look over three of the prettiest little Jeeps to roll out of Detroit!"

"I'm looking for sturdy, Morgan, not just good looking."

He laughed, "Just what Jason here is looking for in a woman, eh Jason?" He said this last while slapping a most uncomfortable looking Sheriff on the back. Gods above, he had an annoying laugh, sort of like a donkey braying, without the cute face. It wouldn't be exaggerating to say I felt I was looking at a gargoyle from the front of a Renaissance Cathedral. He looked like he'd been in some horrendous accident that sheared off his forehead until it slopped like a Neanderthal's, back into a deeply receding hairline of sparse, gun metal grey hair. His dark brown eyes were close set and about as full of warmth as a frozen mudflat. Only his eyebrows looked lively as they were as bushy as two wooly caterpillars and seemed raised in constant wonderment. I was curious how such an unattractive, rather intimidating man could be in sales. *Had to be his winning personality or hopefully some great deals!* I thought, as Jason and I followed what could be the only Troll selling cars in America. *A time of firsts in my life* I thought as I hurried to keep up with his long stride, still feeling a slight tingle in my limbs which I quickly forgot when we got outside.

We left through a side door and when we rounded the corner there she was! A beautiful, cherry red Grand Cherokee. I dismissed the Wrangler beside it when I noticed the soft, easily rent by sharp claws top. It seemed like my fairy godmother had put the GC there just for me. I tried to hide my excitement from Morgan's keen eye as we approached.

"I'd like to see that black Jeep Laredo if I could, Morgan." Jason gave me a quizzical look as he knew the cherry red one was my dream baby. I just wanted to keep Morgan from knowing, as he'd likely jack up the price. It's funny, being rich hadn't changed my attitude toward money. I had my dear dad to thank for that. Since my dad couldn't hold on to money if it was Super Glued to his hand, I grew up knowing the value of things and how to save a dime for tomorrow. There were many nights while I was trying to give my mom some help, I'd wake up grinding my teeth with worry about my own expenses.

My straying attention was brought back to focus when Jason stepped closer and said, "Cathleen, I have to leave you here and get back on the job, but Morgan will get you home."

I didn't much like that prospect, unconsciously moving the fingers on my right hand and turned to Morgan and asked, "Would you mind if I gave the red Grand Cherokee a test drive, Morgan? I think the black one might show the dirt too much."

"Well sure, Cathleen. In fact just keep it for a few days so you can drive around town and get a good feel for how she handles."

I was thrilled with this idea and my smile was even toothier than before. "I'll bring her back by closing time day after tomorrow if that's ok by you."

He seemed delighted at the prospect of a sale and encouraged me to keep the car for the next few days and I was delighted with the chance for warm and convenient 4-Wheel snowy roads transportation.

After thanking Jason for a most enjoyable lunch, we said our goodbyes and I left the dealership in the comfort of a clean vehicle that I planned to make mine. I turned the heater on full blast and was pleased with the speed it warmed the car. I decided to drive over to the radio station and check in with the staff before shopping for groceries. My only real interaction with them had been by email and a one day visit on site to fire the sales manager. I had flown into a small air field and Darla picked me up there and drove me back after the dirty work was done. Not an auspicious beginning, but today was starting to look like the corner was being turned.

I had put my gloves back on after getting into the car and was surprised when I realized my right hand began to feel like I'd left it in the freezer too long. I pulled off my glove and examined it. The fingers were slightly red and tingling, while the palm was almost as red as the Jeep I was driving. Though there was no pain, I started a quick healing spell and watched as the hand returned to a normal, healthy color. *What now?* I wondered. *The only people I had touched with my hand were Jason and Morgan the Giant car salesman; I must be allergic to giants.* I put that thought away for later contemplation and replaced it with a gush of satisfaction as I sighed deeply and drove off in delightful heated comfort.

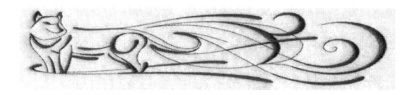

Chapter 8

It's not easy for me to try to charm my way into a tight-knit group, which is what I was bound to find at the station. I have a real aversion to cliques and exclusionary circles like country clubs. Since I'm a nocturnal creature by nature, I find most of these folks don't inhabit my shadowy world anyway. I guess you could say, being a loner was my natural state and I didn't mind my own company. Besides, my dog Ollie was a great listener.

Growing up an only child on a fairly isolated farmstead had its benefits for me, like being the only apple in my parent's eyes. It also had its down-side, like being the only apple in my parent's eyes. While I loved them dearly, my folks were forever trying to control my life and especially my Magic.

Magic, like my beating heart, has been a force in my life from when I was barely able to speak, let alone understand the Wizardry performed on a daily basis by my folks. From lighting the fireplace to chopping the wood for it with just a nod, or a whispered word; things just seemed to happen naturally and with little effort on their part.

My own time as an apprentice to my father was filled with the joy of discovering the powers behind the spells and the fear of the demons and dark ones I would eventually face.

The O'Brien clan, renowned throughout the *Kingdoms of the Green* for their potent Magic was granted increased Magical prowess many centuries ago by the *Guild of the Green Wizards,* *which governed over* all mages in the natural realm.

But nothing is freely given or taken among mystics and mages. In return, even in the face of our own destruction, we O'Briens must use our Magic to protect this world if threatened by any influence from the Dark Realm. Evil beings can be called by wicked Mages to cross over from the Dark Pit of the Sleepless Dead. Here in the natural world these demons can use their considerable power to corrupt and subjugate all that live in the light of the *Green Mother.* Even more frightening, walking among us are humans who would turn to the Dark to gain supremacy over their fellow man. These are demons in human form that approach the unsuspecting with smiles and open hands, but behind the smiles are sharp teeth. And behind the open hand, a killing blow.

My parents pledged their lives as elite *Protectors* in service of the *Green Mother* and were diligent in teaching me their Wizarding skills so I could take my place as a *Protector* in this realm. Unfortunately, they each had their own approach to teaching and doing Magic and this was a source of some heated disagreements around our normally peaceful home. In the end I was allowed to prosper from both my mother's "This and That" brand of magic and my father's more traditional Celtic Magic. Even at my advanced age of twenty-four, I understand I have just scratched the surface of my powers.

Using Magic is like baking a cake, mom always said. "First you put in the right ingredients and all will be well. But one thing out of place, a misspoken word, and you'll likely have a magical flop on your hands." I try hard to avoid the kinds of pitfalls that can occur when a wizard gets too cocky. Dad had a definite opinion for any Mage that didn't study his craft deeply. He always said, "The Wizard who proudly proclaims he is at the height of his art has just stepped off into the abyss." I am careful where I place my feet.

When I pulled into the station parking lot I was struck by the sparse number of cars parked there. *Where the heck was everyone?* I thought. Then I remembered how Prescott, the previous owner, had bragged about running his station on a "*skeleton crew*" after getting rid of some "*dead wood*". It was a huge savings to the station he'd said and "*folks just had to produce more work,*" he explained to me via one of our video conference calls to my lawyer's office. I had since determined we needed at least five new hires to really put together a classy line-up of shows and news segments.

These were well received plans when I contacted the Mayor of Iron Mountain, George Gilbert. New jobs are always a plus to a rural economy and the Mayor praised me for my contribution to his unique community. *Making friends from the top down,* I thought smugly as I grabbed my briefcase. I sighed with regret as I left the warmth of the Jeep and the cold quickly reduced my smug expression to a shiver as I made for the glass front doors of the station, fighting a rising wind that seemed determined to deter my getting inside.

I entered the building through the main lobby to help get a feel for the personality the station radiated. It was painted a pearly grey and covered with plaques awarded to the station for community service, photos of on-air celebrities past and present, past General Managers including Prescott and really horrible water colors depicting what could only have been Iron Mountain before the dawn of man.

My presence was noted while I was making this visual tour, and the receptionist actually blanched when I stated my name.

I didn't quit understand her reaction, but rather enjoyed her falling over herself to welcome me to my new fiefdom. On my quick visit a few months back I had only met with a few people and our receptionist was new to me. She looked like an anniversary edition of a Barbie Doll; with long blond hair and slim figure. Her big blue eyes were now staring at me like she'd just discovered me crawling around under her desk. I quickly said "Sorry to have startled you. I just wanted to drop by and meet some of the staff while I was in town for a few hours."

After much kowtowing (which I also quite liked), I finally got her name and asked that she show me to my office. "Alice," I asked, as we walked up the faux marble staircase to the second floor, "how long have you been at WHIP Radio?"

She replied in a stage whisper that would surely alert her colleagues of my presence. "I've been here for nearly 3 years Miss O'Brien."

"Well," I said, "I hope you can help me adjust to the station's environment since it will be new to me."

"Oh, sure," she said smartly. "We normally keep it at seventy degrees in here." I guess I needed that poke to remind me I wasn't playing ball in the major leagues anymore.

Chapter 9

It took me about an hour to say hello to my new staff as I went department to department. I didn't want to bother them too much as they seemed very busy with their work and pretty stretched to get things done short-handed. I told each of them that I would be holding a full staff meeting on Friday, after we signed off the air, no exceptions for attendance. This put the meeting at ten p.m. I could see this wasn't going to be popular by the eye rolling and the unenthusiastic "oh's," but when I told them there would be pizza they seemed to warm to the idea. After all, it was a Friday night and that's probably what they would be doing anyway.

When I arrived at my office, I sat behind my desk in the rather nice leather, swivel chair and took stock of the people I'd just met. Of course, I had already met with Darla, my new secretary. After her run in with "Mr. Yuck," Darla asked me if I'd consider her switching departments from sales secretary to my personal Administrative Assistant. I jumped at the idea as I found her both competent and mature even though she wasn't much older than I. I needed a steady hand guiding my office life, even if it was a set 70 degrees in here.

Alice seemed well-suited in the receptionist position and I rather liked her perky personality. The fact that she was very pretty helped the otherwise blah aesthetics of the front desk area too. We didn't need a Rhoads Scholar in her position; just home town friendly would serve nicely.

After signing a few papers for purchase approvals, I ventured out of my office again to meet our engineers as they were all tied up with a production schedule earlier. I found we had two full-time staff and one part-time. These three guys were very good at seeming busy. I noticed how they were lounging about their machine-crammed department as if it was a patio with built in fire-pit. They had soda cans everywhere, empty carry-out boxes strewn around the floor in various stages of decomposition, mugs that may have been coffee or the elixir of life the way they cradled them and boxes from the Ugly Baker filled with half-eaten donuts. *At least they seem well fed,* I mused.

"Good morning, gentleman," I said as I stepped into their lair. They jumped up as one, except for the senior engineer. His name was Felix, his co-worker was Jackson. Phil was the part-timer and he was so skittish he seemed to be vibrating in place like an old washing machine. This caused his thick, black-rimmed glasses to slide down his very sharp nose like a toboggan on a slick run. I was certain he'd have a seizure if I didn't leave them quickly.

I surmised from his back being turned in my direction that Felix wasn't too keen on relinquishing any authority to me. He snapped off a quick nod in my direction and kept fiddling with the lighted dials on his console. There was only music playing at the time, a mix of country and quiet rock. He was absorbed in this non-task, while I told the other two about the scheduled meeting for all staff, so I made a point of moving to his side. "I'd like you to make a brief presentation at the Friday meeting, Felix". This got his attention.

"Huh?"

"I want you to explain to the others just what you geeky engineers do in here to make our station function". I said this with a chuckle so they knew I sort of admired the geek in them. "After all, you really are the engine that runs this train, right boys?" They all were quick to agree and smiled as I left them to their cave of lights, knobs and computers, humming their song.

When I returned to my office, I shuffled through my predecessor's over-stuffed file cabinets, looking for personnel records, trying to find out who was making what and who likely needed a raise. I intended to be generous with these workers after what they likely had to endure under Prescott's cut backs and pay freezes, and just his personality for that matter.

I gave up trying to tug files loose after ripping the tops off three of them and decided to let Darla have a go at them later. Sitting back in my chair I began to survey my new domain. The office was painted a soft caramel color and luckily it looked freshly done. The desk was a rich walnut that dominated the room with its size and fine workmanship. Prescott liked the trappings of position I guessed while I squirmed slightly at the thought of him sitting in the chair I now occupied.

I began fiddling with my desk, opening and shutting drawers. When I tried to close the middle drawer tightly, it resisted as if something was blocking it. I removed it after several failed attempts and got down on my knees, feeling around the back of the drawer. Nothing. *Probably a paper clip jamming up the works* I speculated. I had a window directly behind my desk, so the light was fine, but I saw no obstructions. I started to feel the under part of the desk top directly above the faulty drawer. *Bingo!* Whatever it was, it was taped to the wood which seemed more than peculiar to me. *Someone didn't want whatever this is to be found*, I thought.

I began to slowly peel off strips of grey utility tape and when the last of it was removed, I heard a plunk, like metal being dropped on the drawer rails. An old fashioned skeleton key lay in my now gritty palm. As I turned it over a few times to examine it, I felt a chill run down my spine.

My Gaelic instincts pinched my consciousness and I was certain this was not just any forgotten key, hidden away for safe keeping by a paranoid little man; this was going to open the portal to the darkest secrets of Iron Mountain.

I felt my arm and hand begin to stir with that strange tingling sensation I'd experienced earlier after my encounter at the car dealership with Morgan King. Or was it Jason that brought on this strange vibration I wondered. It looked like I had more than one mystery to unlock.

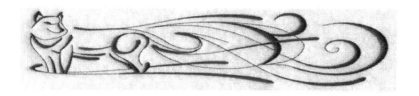

Chapter 10

I left the office by three and because she'd be home until 6:00 p.m. I called my friend Joanie to see how Ollie was doing without his mom.

"Hey, Joanie," how's my baby boy treating you?

"Hey, yourself," she answered. "He's being a perfect gentleman, but he misses his mommy."

I laughed. "I have missed that furry son of mine," I said.

"He'll be very happy to be reunited with you, Cathleen. He hasn't been eating as well and even his walks don't seem to cheer him up much." As a nurse, Joanie was a blessing to me as I knew she'd treat my geriatric dog like the fragile old guy he was and spoil him with attention.

We caught up on some of the gossip swirling around my disappearance from the Pittsburgh scene and laughed over some of the more inventive speculations. One old boyfriend said he knew I was back in Ireland and running a sheep farm with my mom. *Why did I date him again?* One of the on-air personalities from the station said I had opened a microbrewery in Ireland in honor of my father, a well-known stout drinker.

Joanie agreed to meet in two weeks at the airport I'd flown into, as it seemed the only real landmark in the area. She said she'd program the address I gave her into her GPS and be on the road by six in the morning. I voiced my concerns about the coming hard winter weather, but she seemed fine with driving in snow as her four wheel truck was as heavy as a tank. She estimated she'd arrive at the airport by one that afternoon if all went according to plan and Ollie didn't need too many pit stops along the road.

After saying our goodbyes, I realized just how lonesome I actually was in my new home. But like my mom said, there's nothing like a warm bowl of soup to cheer one's spirit. I was crawling around checking out boxes in the kitchen for my favorite chicken noodle, when I heard something. I stopped and listened. There was a distinct sound coming from the second floor. From where I was in the kitchen I determined that there had to be something, or someone in my bedroom. I wasn't particularly brave when it came to confronting dangers of an unknown origin, so naturally I wanted to identify the source of the sound. *Better to hunt down potential dangers before they hunt you down*, I encouraged myself, thinking about the advice my father always preached to me. I screwed up my face, listening hard and there it was again, a soft, muffled, movement above my head. I tiptoed back to where I'd thrown my purse in the living room and retrieved my cell phone. I decided that whatever was up there, I didn't want to face it on my own.

Wanting to prepare myself for any real trouble and remembering all too well the wolf attack of less than a day ago, I spoke the ancient Druid words to get myself ready for this new threat. "Ag-yn-nawd, nerth" "And in protection, Strength."

I felt the hairs on my arms stir as a quick shock of energy traveled up from the floor and through my body. My vision became acutely keen and as I passed my front window I could see the shapes of each snowflake plastered upon the glass. All my senses sprang into a heightened state and I recognized the smell of fur and the sounds of padded paws.

I hurried into a small bathroom off the kitchen and without turning on the light I pressed 911. There was a moment and then, "911 Operator. What is your emergency?"

I whispered, "There's an intruder in my house and I'm alone. Can you send help immediately?" After giving the operator my address, she waited with me on the line until I heard the siren shrieking louder as an emergency vehicle pushed its way through my unshoveled driveway.

"Get to your front door miss and let them in."

Clutching my cell phone, I rushed out of the bathroom. Jason's hand was reaching for the front door knob when I jerked it open and nearly fell into his arms from sheer relief. I wouldn't have to face another attack alone. I wanted to keep more obvious Magic off the radar unless it was absolutely necessary I needed to have a better understanding of just what passed for normal around here before I started shooting *green fire* at it!

"Cathleen, we got your 911 call! Do you know who's in there?" I told him I'd heard someone in my bedroom and had no idea who it might be.

"I keep my doors locked, but most of my belongings are still in theft-ready packing boxes."

I began to follow Jason into the house when he turned and said, "Go wait in my car, Cathleen. I'll go up with Patsy."

"Who's Patsy?" I asked, looking around. Jason held up his gun and smiled that crooked grin.

Chapter 11

"I feel like a real idiot," I began, verbally beating myself up, but Jason stopped me, raising his hand to get my attention.

In a calming voice, he said, "Don't be so hard on yourself, Cathleen. You've only been here a few days and are still shaken up by the other night's experience. I'm sure anyone would be alarmed if they thought there was someone in their house after that."

"Yeah," I agreed without much enthusiasm.

He looked at me with a serious expression and said, "Those raccoons can be very destructive too. Besides, what if it had been a real intruder and you didn't call for help. It's better to be wrong than hurt, or worse." He made sense and more importantly, he was making me feel better about calling in three baby raccoons on a search and destroy mission. They were quite adorable, but Jason said they would bite and wouldn't let me too near. He expertly bagged each one into a burlap sack with the help of his deputy, Leo, who had arrived as back-up a few minutes after Jason.

I was surprised to see Leo, the baker's harassed assistant, wearing a police uniform. He informed me, "I only moonlight at The Ugly Baker, mostly two or three times a week when I work the seven to midnight shift for the Sheriff's Department."

There just wasn't enough law enforcing to go around I guessed.

My little bandits would be set free a few miles from where I lived Jason told me. After saying goodnight he put the squirming mass of burlap into his squad car and drove off with his Deputy not far behind.

After a quick shower, I rechecked my doors and window locks for the third time and taking my cell phone with me went to bed without supper. *Like a bad child who told stories*, I thought to myself, but when I heard the front door rattle in a gust of wind *(must be wind)* I thought , I had to stop myself from dialing 911and making even a bigger pest of myself than the raccoons. Magic is wonderful, but it doesn't compare to a warm smile and a reassuring hug.

I got up around four-thirty the next morning, letting myself sleep in a bit since I'd had such an exciting evening. I didn't have to return to the dealership until six the next evening, so I had almost two days to check out more of the town and its residents. I suspected people would view me as "the newcomer" for years to come in this well-settled community. *The only way to their hearts would have to be through their ears,* I was thinking to myself as I drove east toward the small downtown area and my morning brew.

I need to restock my coffee supply or I'll never make it to work. I'd only been able to manage to pick up a few provisions so I wouldn't starve to death and since I didn't want to live on soup, I intended to go shopping again after lunch.

It was still very dark and mine were the only headlights bouncing off the snowy landscape. With dense forests on either side of the narrow road, I became aware of how claustrophobic I was beginning to feel. I checked to be sure the car doors were locked and switched to the high beams as much as possible, as the heavily falling snow obscured my vision in the brighter lights. The radio was silent as WHIP didn't come on air until six in the morning and with all the interference from the surrounding mountains, there was no hope of reception from outlying stations.

It felt like I was the sole inhabitant of a white universe, a universe I had little connection to. Though I reached out to her, the *Green Mother* was difficult to feel as the roadway slowly blurred under the mask of falling snow.

My scalp began to tingle and I had the creepy feeling that I was being closely watched while I drove at a snail's pace over the unfamiliar snow-covered road. The tree limbs tunneling the roadway shook with each gust of wind, reflecting my own nervous state. Icy crystals blew relentlessly into the narrow beam of my headlights, seeming to shatter like glass upon the piercing yellow shafts.

I kept a close watch on the rear view mirror and my side windows as I snaked my way over the slippery surface. *There! A huge shaggy dog? A wolf? Red glowing eyes?* Whatever it was, I knew it wasn't going to be friendly. I didn't care how slick the road was I pressed down on the gas pedal and gripped the wheel like a beginner with a Driver's Permit. Suddenly fish-tailing, I struggled for control of the wheel. I could feel my tires struggling for traction. I streered toward the less compacted snow, and the 4-Wheel finally kicked in.

As I brought the Jeep out of its side-ways slide, I saw a dark shape stepping out of the shadows and into the pale moonlight at the edge or the woods. I was at a complete stop, the nose of my car pointing into the trees as it approached with a slow, loping gait. If I wasn't hallucinating, I knew its name: *werewolf*!

I began a spell to shield my car. I stared transfixed through my wet windshield at the slowly approaching figure, but as quickly as it appeared, a howl penetrated the dark and it jerked to a stop and retreated back into the cover of the thick trees.

Did I just imagine that? Was that thing called back by some kind of pack leader? Maybe I was just influenced by the silly stories I'd read about this town?

I was frantically considering all the aspects of my latest scare as I got my car pointed into the right direction and resumed my trip toward what I hoped were lots of bright lights and friendly faces.

Early on, when I was investigating the possibility of purchasing WHIP Radio, I'd done an in-depth on-line history search of the town, accessing old newspapers and credible historians. I knew this would be coal country as most of the areas up in these heavily forested mountains were. I'd been amused if skeptical when I ran across several newspaper reports from as far back as 1879 that discussed the local legends. They all speculated on the validity of local accounts of marauding bands of mutant wolves, and most sightings had been centered around the small town of Iron Mountain. People had gone missing and some inhabitants claimed to have seen what they described as a wolf standing on two legs and hunting the heavily forested area around Iron Mountain.

In more recent years, reports of townsfolk and visitors who vanished from trails and cabins in and around Iron Mountain still circulated in the local newspapers and even found their way into papers in the larger cities in the area. The more modern journalists of their times added human interest by mentioning an old Navajo Indian who was suspected of "nefarious deeds" in relation to these disappearances. In the most recent report dated in the 1940s, he was implausibly named again as a suspect in these mysteries and one local was quoted as calling him "the devil's wolf".

His Navajo name was translated into English by the article's author, a renowned anthropologist in Native-American Cultures. The translation from the Navajo was *Joseph Moon Slayer*. After I'd stopped smiling at the eccentricity of backwoods culture, I'd filed this information under crackpot news of the day and forgot about it.

Until now. *I had to pull myself together. If that was what I thought it was I'll need all my powers to protect against another surprise appearance.* With a shrug that ended up being more of a shudder, I refocused my attention to the drive into town.

That worked for about a mile. I was trying to keep myself calm while I watched for any other movement in the woods behind me and was more than relieved to see the light streaming out of the "Ugly Baker's" frosted front window. I pulled into what I guessed was a parking place in front and nearly skipped into the welcoming warmth and sound of human activity.

"Morning, Miss Cathleen." It wasn't Gus who greeted me, but Leo, the gun-toting baker's assistant.

"Leo," I answered, still a bit rattled after my phantom encounter on my drive into town. I managed to smile back at him and say, "I was expecting to see Gus. You off from deputy duty today?"

Leo had frizzy red hair that sat on his head like spun cotton candy, the florescent lighting making it appear almost pinkish. His eyes sagged like an old hound dog after a good chastising, while his mouth seemed to have fewer teeth than a toddler. I could never guess his age, but figured he was somewhat older than Jason.

He was quick to smile back in spite of his lack of pearly whites, and I realized that Leo was a gentle soul who probably enjoyed the bakery much more than the sheriff's squad room. I found myself smiling at this foppish character in his white apron, when Gus came in from the back pantry before he could answer my question.

"Cathleen," Gus said with a warm smile. "Good to have you drop by this morning. Heard you had some furry bandits last night." He chuckled like he'd just won some kind of crazy bet that I'd have another misadventure.

"Guess I'd better get used to how quickly word gets back to you, Gus," I said.

"We like to keep informed when it comes to our town folk, Cathleen. You'll get used to it. It's called caring, and this town's got plenty to go around."

I smiled sheepishly and moved into the store from the doorway where I had stomped my boots clean and taken off my gloves and knit hat. "Gus, if it wouldn't be too much trouble, I think I'd like some fresh coffee with that folksy philosophy." Before I could dig some money out of my pocket, there was a steaming cup of coffee on the counter in front of me. "Thanks," I said grabbing for it greedily and inhaling its creamy, coffee fragrance. "And thanks for remembering that I like my cream heavy."

Gus grinned back at me as he arranged new batches of donuts for the expected early risers. He stopped what he was doing for a moment and looked at me intently, asking, "How you finding your new position at WHIP, Cathleen? Any problems with your staff?"

I took a sip of coffee and said, "I've been generally well received I think. I'm hoping to add to the current staff though, so there will be changes, but I hope for the better"

Gus said, "It would be hard to believe anybody wouldn't like you, Cathleen. I asked because that Prescott guy made some real bone-head moves and was disliked by just about everyone over at WHIP Radio and quite frankly, around town in general."

"I'd like to believe I can keep from making too many bone-head moves, but it'll take time to learn the people working for me there. Guess I can try to buy their loyalty with dozens of donuts from the "Ugly Baker's," right?" I laughed.

"They're some of my most loyal customers," he responded with a chuckle.

Leo had been shuffling the chairs around and sweeping under them in the small eating area, but I noticed he was very much engrossed in my conversation with Gus. At one point he stood by a table and seemed about to say something when Gus yelled over at him to finish up before he sprouted roots at that spot.   I looked over at Leo in time to register a fleeting look of anger cross his face at being scolded. When he caught my eye he flashed me a quick grin and began to move the small tables back into place. As I continued a conversation with Gus, I noticed that Leo kept looking over at me and whenever our eyes connected, he'd shyly look away.

None of this surreptitious star gazing was lost on Gus as he began to chuckle and said to me under his breath, "Looks like you've got yourself an admirer, Cathleen."

I only shrugged and began buttoning my coat and putting on my hat and gloves as I prepared myself for the Arctic blast waiting outside. The last thing I needed was an infatuated groupie; I'd had enough of that sort of unwanted attention in Pittsburgh.

I left the shop with a second cup of coffee and a sweet roll, and for myself, and two dozen donuts to sweeten my arrival at the station. After stowing them on the passenger seat, I jumped back into my already chilly car and headed for work. I thought I'd just check in to see how the staff handled the opening hours of the day. After that, I figured I'd best become a "hunter gatherer" and get some real food in my house since donuts didn't really count as a food group.

In spite of what I now hoped was my over-active imagination, I still looked back into the tunnel of trees I'd just passed through. After a second I said, "Whatever!" and began to drive.

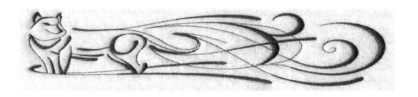

Chapter 12

When I arrived, the sky was beginning to lighten and the sun splashed across the mountain tops, washing the snowcaps with a pearly pink glow. I sighed at the thought of picking up the reigns of my job in semi-darkness, but at least I wouldn't have to be alone in the building. As I trudged through the gloomy shadows, I admitted to myself that I had some hang-over fears from the attack of the dogs, or wolves, or whatever they were. And innocent as it may have been, the invasion of the raccoons didn't help either, not to mention this morning's hairy apparition.

I found Felix at his desk sorting through the day's line-up and ad slots. He looked toward the door when I poked my head in, donut box first. "Hey boss," he said, smiling as he reached into the fragrant treats. "Ready for our meeting Friday?" he asked between bites.

"I was going to ask you the same thing, Felix," I answered.

"I was born ready! Actually, I think I worked out a pretty good presentation for the guys. How long do I have?"

"About 25 minutes this go around. Don't want them to know how to do your job as well as you, do you?" I said laughing.

A few minutes later, Phil, the half-time employee, arrived for his shift. "How about this snow, man," he was saying loudly while shaking off a hat that looked like it once belonged to a Russian Czar. It was obvious he hadn't seen me standing there yet.

"Oh, hey boss."

What's with this "boss thing," I thought, though I was glad my age didn't seem to diminish me as an authority figure. Of course, it didn't hurt that I owned the place.

"Good morning, Phil," I answered. He seemed to withdraw into himself like a turtle into his shell when I looked at him directly. I didn't want to scare him so early in the day with an overflow of energy and turned my attention back to Felix. "Would you give me a run-down on the day's program schedule, Felix? I want to see how the sponsor lineup looks while we're at it too, so I can gauge our sales needs."

Close to 45 minutes and one cake donut later, I left engineering and decided to take a self-directed walking tour to get a fuller picture of the building's nuts and bolts. Plus I needed the exercise to kill my sugar buzz.

After checking out the first two floors and noting where things like the restrooms and supply closets were located, I found the basement door directly off the lobby. I told Alice where I'd be in case of some calamity and then followed dim, over-head lighting down a short flight of stairs. *Have to get brighter lighting down here* I thought. I was glad to find that the furnace and air conditioning units were located near the staircase and happier that they looked practically new. My predecessor was not stingy with the comfort element, just the human one.

I was about to return upstairs after looking quickly through all of the closed off rooms in the front part of the basement, thinking the rest would be more of the same old and broken antenna and radio logs.

Suddenly, the air shifted and I became aware of an animal presence close by. At the same time I picked up a strong and vaguely familiar odor. I inhaled deeply, trying to awaken some memory of where I had encountered something this foul smelling before. On a second deep inhalation I knew with certainty it was the night of the wolf attack.

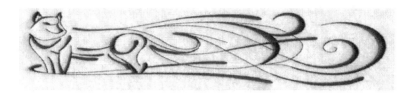

Chapter 13

My heart felt like it would jump out of my body as it slammed into my ribs! I was frozen in place, listening for any growls or scuffing of giant, padded paws. Nothing stirred except my pounding pulse. Instinctively, I looked around for some kind of weapon so I could defend myself. I didn't want to call upon my magic because the staff was beginning to arrive and anyone looking for me down here would probably not understand why my fingertips were shooting green fire or electrical surges. There was nothing remotely resembling a weapon except a few bent radio antennas and I seriously doubted I could defend myself with something so light it would bend like a willow branch. I reached into my pockets as a last resort and found the skeleton key I'd discovered hidden in the desk. I'd slipped it back into my pocket this morning on a whim, thinking I might have time to locate the door it fit. Then a thought hit me. *What if this fits some door down here?* I realized I had to rely on my training as a Mage since there was no other source of protection and just hope none of my staff would venture down here and witness what I couldn't really explain.

Since I didn't detect any movement in the shadowy recesses of the basement, and my sensitized skin surface didn't scream imminent *danger*, I decided to search for the source of the smell. By now, I believed the pungent odor came from one of the back rooms. As quietly as I could, I continued down the poorly lit hallway. On either side at various intervals, I noted more closed rooms and the odor of wild animal increased with each step. Still, I heard no sound, or muffled animal noises.

I had been told when I purchased the station that this lower part of the building had once housed the town jail back in the 1800s. *These must have been cells down here,* I thought as I slowly moved deeper into the increasing darkness. While the smell got stronger, so did my state of awareness as I knew I had to be getting to the back-end of the basement any minute. Meaning whatever I smelled was back there waiting quietly in the near darkness.

As I rounded a corner at the end of the hallway, I peered into the murky shadows where the weak light barely seemed to penetrate. Chanting softly, I said the words that would draw upon the darkness to cover me like a cloak and conceal my presence, "*Nasc Scath*" I repeated the words and they seemed to bounce off the thick miasma of stench as I moved forward. The shadows were now bound together in a perfect blanket for concealment. Just as I was preparing to move further into the gloom and before my body was completely enveloped in this magical camouflage, my shoulder was gripped by a huge hand that broke my concentration and the spell was shattered like safety glass hit by a bullet. My scream was ear-shattering even to me, and I hoped to the great ogre that had me in a vise grip.

Before I could escape I was roughly spun around and there, looming over me was Morgan King. He had a flashlight in one hand and my arm in the other. "You scared the holy crap out of me, Morgan!" I threw my head back and was yelling into his face while I disengaged from his iron grip.

"I'm really sorry, Cathleen," he said in a contrite voice. His flashlight was emphasizing his misshapen face, making him seem as frightening as what I suspected lay behind the door. "Tell me what you think you're doing down here anyway?" I said peevishly.

"I came looking for you as a matter of fact. I thought I'd bring the papers on that Jeep you've been driving around town and see if we could close some kind of deal. Your receptionist told me I'd find you here."

"And you couldn't wait until I came back upstairs? You must be awfully anxious to sell." That sounded a bit harsh even to my ears so I added, "I do want it though, for a good price of course."

"So why *are* you creeping around in the basement, Cathleen? It looked like you were waiting to discover some vampire coffin or something." He gave a short chuckle, to lighten the atmosphere I suspected.

I wasn't sure I wanted to share my thoughts on the wolf smell as it was probably just mildew and musty wood that set me on the scent. "I was trying to see just what's stored down here and thought I heard something."

"That would have been me I expect. I'm not the lightest on my feet," he said. Suddenly, he stood very still and began to sniff the air like a hound. "Pretty strange smell, don't you think?" I looked closely at him and realized he was facing the last door at the end of the hall. He moved forward a foot and then another. He looked immobile, rigid, almost like a hunting dog on point. "I think we need to go back upstairs *now*, Cathleen."

I was gripping the key and moved next to him. "I found a key, Morgan, and thought I'd try this door. It looks very old and the key might fit."

Morgan quietly asked me, "Are you sure you want to check that now?"

"Sure," I replied, sounding more confident than I felt just then.

He moved closer to me and stretched out his hand palm up. "OK, but I think you might want to let me go first after we get it opened up." I placed the skeleton key in his huge hand where it looked tiny like something Alice would have used in Wonderland. He inserted it smoothly into the lock on the door. It turned. Slowly he turned the knob, and pushing the door open a hair. The odor was almost overpowering and we both gagged in response.

When the door was pushed further inside the room we both saw what looked like an indoor stable. Hay was spread around the room and large, empty bowls were flung about as if tossed when emptied of food. Peering into the flashlight's circles we saw what appeared to be two shaggy coats lying in a heap in one corner of the room. Then the coats stirred and four red eyes were fastened on us like flies on a corpse.

They never growled or moved. It was as if they were expecting us or maybe they were just full and didn't need to eat us. Whatever it was we were not hanging around to find out. Using his flashlight like a cattle prod, Morgan pushed me back into the dark hallway. I had to use all my will power not to begin a ward which is a natural response we magic users experience when confronted with extreme danger. The two monsters that were now stirring inside that pit looked like a nightmare from my Night Crawlers show. If someone had called them in to me on air, I would still be laughing. Too bad I wasn't laughing now.

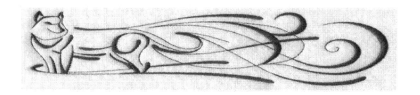

Chapter 14

Without a moment's hesitation, Morgan slammed the door shut and we both backed away. Though his face seemed etched in the horror we just witnessed together, I couldn't shake the feeling that those creatures somehow knew Morgan was no threat. Maybe it was the way they just stared over at him, almost in anticipation, but certainly not as if they were stirring themselves to charge him.

For myself, I felt like the last passenger on the Titanic to see the iceberg. "What in the name of all that's holy was THAT?" I whispered, as if my voice would stir them to immediate violence. Morgan's breathing had become labored, like he'd run a marathon. I asked him again, louder this time, "Morgan, do you have any idea what's living in the basement of my radio station?"

He turned slowly toward me and answered softly, the whole time pulling me further away from the door with little tugs on my arm "I'm hoping that what we just saw were a couple of over-sized pit bulls, but in truth I believe you already met at least one of these boys a few nights back.

I took a moment to process what he said and then I realized that he was very likely correct. "I didn't realize you knew about that encounter. But it still doesn't explain what they hell those, those beasts are doing in my station's basement, behind a locked door for which I apparently have a key."

"Cathleen," he was saying between slightly yellow clenched teeth, "what we have here is a problem that I thought was taken care of years back when I was a kid in Iron Mountain."

I began unconsciously backing away from him and the door when I bumped against the wall. Morgan came toward me. "Let's get away from this area so I can explain a few things to you about our town."

"I'm sure it's very interesting, but what the hell are we going to do about that," I exclaimed, pointing at the door.

Without turning our backs to the secret monster motel in my station's basement, we had both started moving toward the stairs and better lighting. Morgan gripped my elbow to speed our distance from the dreadful holding cell. I felt the same chill run up my arm that I had experienced back at the car dealership. *Alarm bells were ringing in my head so loudly I could barely focus on what Morgan was saying.*

"They can't get out. We probably need to give the sheriff a call. I have no idea why they are here, or how they got here. No idea. It was supposed to be over twenty years ago," he said in hushed tones.

"What was over twenty years ago?"

"That's what I was trying to explain. Iron Mountain was having visitors again after a long dry spell. Folks like to do the trails here a-bouts, or fish in Iron Lake for trout and such. We had money coming into the town and were planning to build a new hotel. Then it started, vanishing tourists and soon, even missing town's people."

"I read about the legends, but are you saying those evil dog-like creatures are responsible for those missing persons? That's crazy."

"Believe me," he said softly, "it's not crazy. When the old Sheriff, Jim Dugan, starting digging into the disappearances, he didn't find a trace of the people who had gone missing. It was as if they had never existed, or been swallowed up by the mountain,"

Morgan was still moving toward the stairway as he continued, "Some of the relatives of the missing tourists came up here to do their own investigating, or they sent private detectives, but no one was able to solve the mystery of the disappearances and some of the investigators never made it back down the mountain. Pretty soon word got out in various news articles and people stopped coming here to hike or visit. It was like we had the plague and the town pretty much dried up."

If he was trying to scare me more than I already was, he made some progress. We continued our conversation in hushed tones, as if the abnormal animals would break out and devour us if we disturbed them further.

"But you said some of the town's people had gone missing too. Wasn't there any trace of *them*? Surely the locals would be searching the woods and mountains until they found *something*!"

Morgan looked intently at me for a second as if he was considering whether or not to share more information with me. He said, "Cathleen, Jason Tate's little brother was one of those missing persons and with both his parents gone by then, Jeff was all the family Jason had."

I took in this information and tried to picture how devastated Jason must have been. "I have no family," he had told me during our lunch. I had felt a tiny chill when he said that as I thought it sounded almost as if he were more angry than sad.

I had been listening to this explanation as I strained to hear anything from the room with what I thought of as the "Demon Dogs."

I asked Morgan for the key that he just used to open the door to that nightmare and he handed it over with some reluctance. "I hope you aren't thinking of going back in there, Cathleen. You are no match for those creatures."

"I have no intention of going into that room without the law, Morgan. Right now, we need to make sure the door is locked and stays that way." I took the key and moved quietly back to stand in front of the door, inserted it once more into what I noted seemed a well-oiled lock face. *Hmmm, I thought. This door seems ancient and yet the lock appears to be fairly new.*

I felt more than heard a motion behind me and turned in time to see Morgan moving as quietly as a shade at a seance, back up the stairs. *So much for not being light on his feet,* I thought as I more or less ran after him in a more undignified retreat. Whatever we had just encountered down in the dark I knew I couldn't use my magic with witnesses around. That made me more than a little nervous and got my legs pumping like a sprinter. *Maybe I'll be in shape to run with Jason after all* I thought, grimly taking the stairs two at a time.

Chapter 15

We both made the first floor landing and burst through the stairwell door. "Hey there." It was Alice, our receptionist, smiling automatically like some ever cheerful Miss Congeniality before she began to take note of our less than friendly demeanors. "Is there something wrong, Ms. O'Brien? I only ask because you both sort of look like you shook hands with a ghost down there."

Her chuckle was cut short when I blurted out, "Who has access to the basement, Alice?"

She stopped grinning long enough to ruminate for a minute. And squinting her baby blues with the effort said "Why, that would be Ed Porter, our janitor and, on occasion, the furnace and air conditioning guy. It's really kind of spooky, so no one wants to go down there unless we have to. Oh, and Mr. Prescott, our previous owner, used to store some stuff he hunted with down there I think. I saw him take one of those fancy bows down once. And he'd keep the deer or whatever he shot, down there in the basement freezer. I saw him bring in brown packages that looked like the kind the butcher sells." She seemed exhausted by this monologue and smiled her dimpled-cheek smile once more and returned to her desk before I could question her further, or she collapsed with the effort.

I turned to Morgan who was pale but not panting like a long distance runner and said softly, "Morgan, I'm calling Jason Tate to report those things in the basement. We'll need a vet or some kind of animal handler to tranquilize them before we can have them removed." Morgan was silent and staring into the distance. "Morgan, did you hear me? We need help with this!" He was still unresponsive except for a grunt that might have been a "yes" and I called over to Alice. "Alice, would you please get Sheriff Tate on the phone for me?"

She looked alarmed and shot a quick look at Morgan, but quickly answered, "Of course Ms. O'Brien." When I looked back at him, Morgan seemed recovered from his initial shock as he said loudly, "Perhaps we could retire to your office, Cathleen, and get back to the purchase of that beautiful vehicle you've been driving."

I was certain all this flowery stuff was said to put Alice at ease and I appreciated Morgan's efforts. It wouldn't do for word to start circulating around the station about wild beasties living under their feet!

When he was seated across from me at my desk, Morgan seemed to have regained most of his composure as he asked, "Cathleen, I think we should get the car deal behind us so we can concentrate on the recent discovery."

I was somewhat unprepared for the switch in gears from terrified woman to happy consumer, but I realized that Morgan might have needed to focus on something he understood rather than the two carnivores below us.

He continued, "What do you say to $25,000 on the Jeep and I'll throw in a new stereo system to sweeten the deal."

"I'll take it for $20,000, Morgan, and pay in full today." His eyebrows shot up with surprise, causing a great, furry ruffle to form across his sloping forehead. He seemed quite happy though to have concluded our negotiations so quickly.

"Done," he said, smiling broadly. "For such a young lady, you certainly have your head on straight."

I smiled and thought inwardly, *I'm just happy it's still attached to my shoulders.*

I signed off on the paperwork and just as I was finishing up my phone rang. "Hi, heard you wanted to speak with me." Jason seemed a no frills on the phone kind of guy. I told him I would appreciate if he could come to the station this evening around seven and would he try to bring the local Animal Control officer, or maybe even a vet.

"Care to give me more details, Cathleen?" he asked calmly.

"Well," I said and then got up to close my office door. "When I was checking out the station's basement area, I found what looks like a holding pen for wild wolf-type dogs, only they're gigantic! I know it sounds crazy, but Morgan King is here and he saw them too." I sounded a little hysterical to myself, but I hoped Jason wouldn't think I'd gone too deep into the woods. When I glanced over at Morgan he was watching me intently from under hooded eyes. He was either dozing off or scrutinizing my every word.

"I'm coming over now, Cathleen. Under no circumstances are you, or any of the staff, to go back to that room. "He sounded almost upset, but I sensed it wasn't with me. I assured him that would be the last thing I'd want to do. I asked Morgan if he'd wait until the Sheriff came and investigated the mystery below so that he could give his own impression of what we both saw. Again, I sensed some reluctance, but after much hemming and hawing, he agreed.

"It's kind of hard to make sense of this, Cathleen," Morgan was saying, as he gathered up his paperwork and stuffed it into his jacket pocket. "I know that Jason always said wild wolves didn't carry off those people years back, but now that we've discovered these monstrous wolf-like things, he may have to re-think his theory." He let out a long sigh and continued. "I've always believed that's why Jason took the job of Sheriff of Iron Mountain. He's determined to uncover what he calls "the truth to end it all." For a breath of a second, I thought I saw his full lips quirk into a smile.

I thought for a moment and asked, "I know you said authorities and towns people searched in the woods and mountain areas around here, Morgan, but has anyone ever checked out the Iron Mountain Coal Mine? And why do you think those monsters are in the station's basement? Who would have put them there and why are we just discovering them?"

"Whoa! Too many questions for me, Cathleen," he said, waving me off with those huge hands of his. "I have no answers, only questions like you."

He continued in a subdued voice even though my door was closed. "That old mine was shut down after the last big cave-in, in 1943 or '44. That killed over 20 miners. It really devastated the town they say. There were so many dead that the local undertaker couldn't handle the bodies and had to ship some in ice trucks to the next town over. So many dead, it truly boggles the mind." He sighed and leaned back in the chair.

Morgan seemed spent by the events known and unknown, so I suggested we go to the break room on the first floor for coffee and if we were lucky, a stale donut from the box I saw on the table earlier. *That was before this turned into a Friday the 13th horror show!* I thought bleakly.

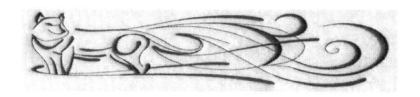

Chapter 16

Jason must have been in the neighborhood because he arrived before my coffee had time to cool. Morgan seemed relieved to see him.

"Jason," he said with a tight smile on his face as he stood to greet him. "We sure are happy to see you buddy!"

"Would you like to tell me exactly what you and Cathleen saw in that room, Morgan?" Jason asked in a steady voice. He sat at the table with us as Morgan described the jumbo-sized doggies and I added the putrid odor and fiery red eyes they turned on us.

"Jason," I added with real concern, "this is not something my staff needs to be aware of yet, is it? I don't want them scared out of their wits." He turned that one beautiful green eye toward my face and said in a quiet, steady voice, "Cathleen, you'll need to cancel any plans you've made here until we can clear out the critters, or I can't guarantee the safety of your people."

This made sense even though I was reluctant to throw everyone into a tizzy due to an interrupted work day. "I'll have Darla put out an email to the staff, that meetings and any shift changes are on hold until further notice."

"Good, now, is there some way you can run this place remotely? I want to clear the building until we know what we're dealing with."

I hadn't expected a full-fledged evacuation, but reflecting back to those evil eyes and vile smell, I saw the wisdom in that action. "I'll get with my head engineer. Give me 15 minutes."

As I started to leave the break room I turned back to see Jason and Morgan in a huddle of hushed conversation. Even from that distance I could see that Jason was very tense and his face held a look of determination.

They both seemed agitated when I got back to them. I announced the station was going to run music and old shows until it signed off at 10:00. "What should I tell my people?"

Morgan interrupted before Jason could respond. "Tell them they are getting a half-day because of the hard work they've been doing."

I left them standing there again and returned to my office where I spoke to my staff over the intercom. I heard cheers and whistles and a few "Go Boss" chants. *Guess Morgan knows people*, I thought.

It took the better part of an hour before all the staff was clocked out. Engineering had programmed the necessary equipment to keep airing shows and music until the 10 P.M. sign-off hour. Jason checked all the doors to the various offices and closed any that remained open. He also closed off the break room, even switching off the lights. *How long will we be under lock-down* I wondered to myself as I scanned my now darkened radio station.This was definitely not a great start to my new job as head honcho here. I thought back to one of dad's favorite sayings about new beginnings. "Life is a circle of experiences and no matter where you find yourself, you've already been there." My dad was a rather unique thinker, according to my mother.

We were standing in the reception area watching staff leave for the day and making sure they were all accounted for. Jason must have read my mind or maybe the forlorn look on my face as he turned to me and said, "We'll work as quickly as we can, Cathleen, to get your station back to normal." I smiled weakly at him and was just about to say "great" when we heard what sounded like a scream of pain followed by a growl that made the hairs on the back of my neck stand up and salute my ears.

Jason was a blur of motion and before I could move he'd already crossed to the basement door behind us. "Jason!" I yelled frantically. "Wait until we can get the Animal Control people here!"

"I *am* the Animal Control people!"he yelled back as he pulled his revolver out of his holster.

Morgan and I ran toward the door only to have it slammed in our faces. Jason's muffled voice called out "Don't open this door until I tell you to."

No way, I thought grimly. I wasn't going to let him face those beasts alone. I left Morgan standing by the door with an anxious look on his scary face. I raced back to Engineering and found the jumbo-size flashlight I'd seen on Phil's desk. I couldn't call up a flame in my hand as I had witnesses to my Magic at the moment. *What good is my Magic* I thought with rising frustration. I noticed a long pole they had in there to open and shut the high windows in their offices. Grabbing it, I spun on my heal and raced back the way I had come.

There was a loud bang from below that sounded like the old gun my dad used to hunt rabbits in the hills around our old farm house. Running back to where I'd left Morgan, I asked, "Did you hear a shot? When he nodded, staring helplessly at the closed door, I pushed past him.

"I'm going down there, Morgan. He'll need help and at the very least, he'll need this!" I said as I held up the flashlight. With that I opened the door a fraction, straining to see past my light into the inky pools of darkness.

As I started down the first step, I felt Morgan touch my shoulder and say, "Give me the pole, Cathleen. I think I may be a tad stronger than you in a fight." I relinquished my would-be sword and let him lead the way.

I was wishing I could safely cast a spell without being detected when judging by the way Morgan jumped, we heard it at the same moment, a deep grunt. Then I smelled the now familiar odor of shaggy beast. We froze on the last step while I used the flashlight like a fan, waving it back and forth, trying to capture the source of the sound in the tiny beam of light. There, huddled on the floor near the second storage room, was one of the giant creatures. Its fur was matted and streaked with clots of what looked like dried mud. His head was resting on a paw the size of two baseball mitts. The only time I had seen a head close to that size was on the grizzly bear at the Pittsburgh Zoo.

"Dear gods above," I breathed out in a gush of air like I'd been hit in the stomach. Without moving his head, the giant beast turned his demon-red eyes upward to see us and then without further ado rolled over onto its side.

Both Morgan and I stood like enchanted statues. Finally, I whispered "Do you think he's asleep?"

"Nope," he answered in hushed tones, "I think he's dead." Before I could put a toe on the cement floor, we heard a second shot ring out from the end of the hallway. We tiptoed past the big body sprawled out in front of us and giving it a wide birth we ran down the corridor toward the room that had served as the beasts' kennel. Jason was inside the fetid smelling cell with his gun still in his hand.

"You don't like to follow orders do you, Cathleen?" he asked softly. But I'd seen the look of concern for me on his face and I didn't feel scolded. I felt cared about.

"We couldn't let you face them alone." I said with as much spunk as I could muster.

"There were just the two of them, Jason," Morgan was saying loudly as if his relief was amplifying his volume.

Morgan was looking at the second fallen animal and shaking his head. "Jason, who's been feeding these monsters and better still, what was he feeding them? Good grief man, these things are nightmare creatures from some other planet!"

Jason walked over to Morgan and placed his hand on his friend's burly shoulder saying, "Morgan, let's not get too worked up here. I'm going to start by investigating everyone who comes into this place, from employees to workmen. We'll get our answers."

Morgan didn't seem convinced, but didn't push it any further. I decided to ask Jason the nagging question bumping around my head like a pin ball. "Jason, is it possible these beasts have something to do with the disappearances of the people around here in past years?"

He took a quick look at Morgan who gave a little shrug. "Guess you know more of Iron Mountain's history than I credited, Cathleen." He turned away from us without answering and putting his gun back into the holster said, "Let's get back upstairs where we can breathe some fresh air."

"Jason!" I hadn't moved. "How did the beast in the hallway die? Did you shoot it?" Jason shook his head, no.

"There was someone else down here. Someone who disappeared like smoke in the wind when he heard me coming. All I saw was what appeared to be a huge swirl of dust and then it vanished."

"But how did he get to the animals? I left that door locked," I said "and I still have the key." I had reached into my pocket and produced the skeleton key.

"There has to be another way to access these rooms down here without being seen. Believe me, we will be conducting a thorough search and will find any secret passageway. For right now, let's go back upstairs so I can call for backup." I immediately thought of Deputy Leo, the baker's assistant and hoped he wasn't the only help we could call in.

When we entered the upstairs lobby, the building seemed unnaturally quiet. *Well of course it's quiet, everyone went home* I thought and felt a little embarrassed by the chill that went through me as I looked around. The Demon Dogs were dead and couldn't do us any harm. But I kept feeling like we weren't safe yet. There was the matter of *who* was keeping them and *why*. *Not to overlook the fact that they were here, in my radio station, munching on a high protein diet no doubt. These creatures were not your garden variety mongrels. They were tailor made by someone to undertake some really nasty commands. Was eliminating me one of those commands?*

Jason insisted on doing an immediate and thorough search of the basement so called his Deputy, Leo, and told him to get over to WHIP Radio right away. He also instructed him to bring the darts and tranquilizer gun he kept locked in his office for animal emergencies. He told Leo where to find the key to the closet where everything was stored and to bring two extra-large body bags from the morgue on his way here. I had some serious doubts that Leo could handle these complex orders, but less than 40 minutes later he was standing in front of the station with a trunk full of the requested items. I was beginning to believe I had misjudged Leo's abilities based on appearance alone. I considered that I may have been making poor judgments all along. *After all, what do I really know about any of these people?* That sounded paranoid even to me. *I need some time to process this.* I made an excuse about using the rest room and went back down the hall. When I was out of sight of the three men, I scooted into my office.

I knew that the quickest way to pandemonium was to allow chaos to jumble clear thoughts and insights. My dad often said to me in his soft Irish brogue, "Never let your mind get bedazzled by facts lass, when fiction will do nicely." Right now there were only a few facts to consider, the reports of missing people from the 1800s to about 20 years ago, and the discovery of two wolf-like beasts in the basement of the station. *Has it really been less than a week since I moved here?* As I sat behind my desk thinking, I reflected on the kennel below my feet. *Hey!* I sat up straight in my chair. *What if those beasts were actually like guard-dogs. Maybe they were protecting something or someone. Perhaps they were killed because it was too dangerous to continue to keep them here.* And *maybe the previous owner of the station is the person to answer these questions.* This seemed a reasonable assumption since he brought game he hunted to the basement for storage, or was it to feed his menagerie?

I pulled open the desk drawer where I had found an old staff directory: **Malcom Prescott General Manager/Owner.** I jotted down his number and hoped he still lived in the area. With that I quickly returned to the men who hardly seemed to have noticed my absence as they were setting up their equipment, including the tranquilizer gun, and what looked like a ray gun from a bad Godzilla movie.

I walked over to Jason and said, "If you don't mind, Jason, I think I'd like to get some work done in my office so things run smoothly when we go back on air."

He looked at me for a moment like he was weighing the truthfulness of this statement before answering, "Sure, Cathleen. We'll be awhile though so if you wanted to go home I'll understand." I assured him I was there until they finished investigating. With that he turned back to his work and I returned to my office to call Malcom Prescott.

I hoped he'd remember me as he always seemed to have trouble with my name during our phone negotiations. *He was so distracted during those calls* I remembered. I wondered if he knew about the inhabitants below. *A curious bonus to the sale,* I thought with a small shiver.

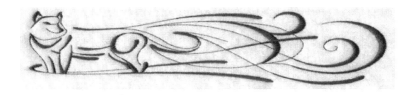

Chapter 17

Prescott answered the phone on the second ring. I couldn't believe it. It was so unexpected that I sat frozen for a second after he spoke. "Hello?" His voice held a slight stuttering sound I didn't remember from previous phone conversations.

I got my head together and said, "Mr. Prescott, this is Cathleen O'Brien. I purchased your radio station several months ago." He didn't respond, but I thought I heard a moan and a chair scrape across the floor followed by a thud as he likely sat down.

"I remember you, Ms. O'Brien. What can I do for you?" He asked this without much warmth.

I took a breath and said, "Mr. Prescott, there has been a rather strange discovery at the station. Since you are still in the area, I'd appreciate the opportunity to speak with you personally about the ramifications."

"What *kind* of discovery? I can't be responsible for any structural problems, Ms. O'Brien," he replied gruffly.

I didn't want to share the story of the wild beasts in the basement as I'd come to think of them, so I said, "It's a matter of some delicacy and I really am not at liberty to discuss it over the phone. Can we get together this evening perhaps?"

There was a long silence and I thought he must have hung up on me when he said tersely, "My place at eight, Ms. O'Brien." With that, he did hang up and left me holding the phone. *Darn*, I thought. *He didn't even give me directions.*

I decided I'd better leave the house very early so I could give myself time to get lost as I inevitably do in strange places. After explaining to Jason that I was going home to do some unpacking I said my goodbyes and left the station. Jason had seemed relieved when I said I was leaving as I'm sure he felt I would get in the way of their search. Also, his look told me he was concerned for my safety which made me feel better about going.

I programmed Prescott's address into my GPS after copying it out of the staff directory and left the house as dark was just creeping into the woods around my garage. I felt a distinctive shift in the frigid air, then the crisp sound of a foot on the frozen crust of the snow as I opened the door to my Jeep. Taking a quick breath, I went rigid, every muscle ready to snap into action in the next instant.

"Hi there, Miss Cathleen," came a high-pitched voice from behind me.

I jumped like someone had zapped me with a taser, and with a burst of expelled   air said, "Leo, I didn't hear you, or your patrol car for that matter. What are you doing here?" I closed the car door while asking this, thinking he wouldn't ask where I was going.

"I came over to check up on you for the Sheriff. He couldn't come himself because he's been searching the basement over at the station since you left earlier. This certainly is a strange business, isn't it?" I had never noticed before that Leo spoke pretty well for what passed as the "dumber" of dumb and dumber, around here. I also noted that his red mop of hair was now combed neatly and likely had hair product in it to keep it from springing wildly from his head the way I remembered it. He seemed different in other ways too, more poised and self assured.

"May I inquire where you might be going, Miss Cathleen? I know for a certainty that the Sheriff wants you to stay at home, indoors, until he can sort things out over at WHIP."

"I don't plan on staying in my house until this is "sorted out", Leo. In fact, I need a few items and am going out for a short time. Please tell the Sheriff I'm just fine if he's concerned and will speak with him in the morning."

"May I ask where you will be, Miss Cathleen? Just so I can let the Sheriff know in case he needs you back at the station."

"As I said, I need a few things for the house. And Leo, I don't have to check in with the Sheriff." I said this rather stiffly because he implied that I needed some kind of travel permit. With that, I got into my Jeep and left him standing there in the snow with a sad look on his long face.

I felt rude for running off like that on Leo, but I really didn't want to stand around talking with him when I needed to get on the road. As I backed out of my driveway, I noticed Leo's squad car was nowhere in sight. Before I could sort the mystery out of how he'd arrived at my place, I heard the first instructions from my friendly GPS and forgot to be concerned about yet another mystery

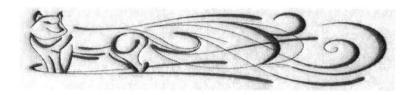

Chapter 18

Prescott lived less than an hour away according to my calculations, but that was with good road conditions. *I hate these curvy roads,* I thought as I picked my way through the slippery, snow-covered twists and turns. I had had to call the Chamber of Commerce for Iron Mountain to get proper directions as my GPS couldn't supply the information on the rugged back roadways.

After I exited off the highway out of town, I was navigating with the hand written directions from some lady named Dorothy at the Chamber. I quickly missed the soothing companionship of my GPS talking me through to my destination. In what felt like hours later, my directions confirmed that I was finally nearing my destination.

The house was dark when I finally located it at the end of a natural cul-de-sac. There were only two other houses in the area and they were spread out over deeply wooded acres. I turned into what passed for his driveway, thankful I'd chosen a Jeep as my mode of mountain transportation and parked beside an old Land Rover, snuggled under almost a foot of snow. In fact, the lack of any tire tracks on the pristine landscape indicated Prescott hadn't moved this vehicle in quite some time. Even accounting for the recent snows, the whole area looked untouched except for what appeared to be several kinds of animal prints and scattered litter from the trees. I sat in the Jeep studying the rustic landscape.

When I got out and shut my car door it sounded like a shotgun blast in the stillness of the shadowed night that seemed to gather like a chill shroud around me. I could see a few lights on in the neighbor's houses, but they were distant and seemed inaccessible. A shudder passed through my body, from more than the freezing temperature. I couldn't shake the feeling I wasn't alone in the deserted snowdrifts, which kept my eyes darting around like a deer in hunting season.

Prescott's house had been swallowed by the deep gloom. Hulking evergreens loomed like sentinels above the roof. Their long furry branches sagged under the weight of the snow and scraped against the roof with every wind gust, making a weird scratching sound against the rough shingles. My already taut senses screamed when I stepped onto the creaky wooden porch. The entrance structure seemed to be returning to the earth in stages, as it sagged dangerously toward its rotting middle boards. There were drifts of snow piling against pieces of wicker furniture that appeared to have grown roots where they stood, as tendrils of fiber hung down from what were once seats and chair backs. The front door was slightly ajar and I leaned forward to call in. "Hello, Mr. Prescott. It's Cathleen O'Brien."

When there was no answer and no sound of footsteps, I tried again. No response. I thought he might be in the back of the house so I began to work my way around to a back door, tripping over hidden tree roots the size of a man's arm. I used the wood siding on the house to help steady my footing as the low hanging trees blotted out any light from the night sky.

When I finally found the door leading to what was his kitchen area, I thought I saw something move to my left. I jerked my hand away from the door knob and stared into the shadows among the trees. Nothing moved and I told myself it was probably a coyote, or fox, or just my jumpy nerves. But my inner alarm system told me otherwise. I couldn't see who or what had triggered my hyper sensitivity, but I knew I was being stalked.

And there was a new smell mixed in with the fresh pine of the evergreens, a heavy, musky scent. I continued to stare into the slightly swaying trees.

Finally, seeing nothing I turned back again to the door and as I turned the knob, realized it was unlocked. I opened it and with my head poked inside the darkened room, I called out again for Prescott. "Mr. Prescott, I'm coming in." I let my eyes adjust to the ambient light provided by the digital displays on his stove and microwave. *Where is he? And what is THAT!*

There was a flat pool of black, inky matter between the kitchen table and the door. I didn't want to touch it, or *anything* for that matter. *This might be a crime scene* I thought calmly. I surprised myself at the steadiness of my reaction. I stepped gingerly around the curious puddle and left the kitchen stepping into a passageway with two rooms off to the side. One was clearly a bathroom and had no sign of Prescott. The next was a small living room with another source of light from the face of a clock-radio. It was close to our meeting time of eight P.M.

I stood next to what might have been an expensive leather chair once. Now it looked decidedly like an implement of torture with the springs poking through the seat and pieces of a heavy corded rope hanging from what had been the carved wooden arms.

Prescott couldn't be called a warm person by any stretch of kindness, but he seemed meticulous in his dealings and record keeping. When we had our two conference calls, he was well-spoken and might even be called prissy in his speech. This house certainly didn't reflect the person I thought he was.

As I left the living room I saw a staircase, its varnished surface glowing faintly in the dim light. I didn't really want to continue my search for Prescott, but felt some concern for his safety since I had asked him to meet me there. I overruled my prickly skin warnings and began to climb the creaky stairs. At the top, I found myself across from three rooms and another bath.

Pushing gently on a partially opened door, I stepped into what turned out to be a sparsely furnished bedroom with a single, neatly made bed, a wooden chair and a small dresser. There were no pictures of family or art work hanging on the walls.

After studying a jacket I saw hanging from the chair back I became aware of some kind of dull glow that was helping to light the area. Looking up I saw a map of the nighttime sky as it would appear over this region, illuminated with carefully applied glow in the dark paint. The planets with their appropriate moons, hung suspended in place by unseen wires. As I craned my neck to study this creative display, I recognized the Milky Way and the other constellations from my times observing the star flung skies with my father. He was keen on having me read the "Dome of Life" as he called it, so I could understand the sacred cycles of beginnings and endings. Now I was wondering who'd been looking up at this display and what beginnings and endings had they envisioned?

I was peering up at what was decidedly a bizarre room decoration for a fifty-year-old man, when I felt the air in the room shift. My father, as a Master Celtic Mage, was trained in the more arcane forms of survivalist techniques. Early on in my training, he taught me how to detect subtle changes in room temperatures, using the exposed surface of my skin as a sensor to changes in heat and cold. I also learned to detect movement under water that didn't stir the surface above, things that only those initiated into the ancient cults of Druid Celtic lore would understand and practice. By the time I was 12, my very skin had become a tool in these arts and now, my body tingled and the fine hairs on my neck and arms stirred.

I spun around and saw Prescott standing four feet away from me. I recognized him immediately from our teleconference calls. But this was a very different man altogether. His eyes blazed a deep red and his hairy hands clutched a double-headed ax. I took in a sharp breath of the stale air and began to chant an ancient Celtic prayer to ward off the evil eye and protect against evil doers. My father always assured me of its power to keep me safe. I hoped it would be as effective on a nasty werewolf, because now I knew that was what stood before me.

Prescott's face was covered in a thick mat of brown fur making his eye glasses seem ludicrous, like they'd been painted on by a cartoonist. He was hunched over and I could see more fur bristling over the top of his shirt collar and in stiff brown tuffs from his unbuttoned shirt front. I wasn't sure if his teeth were yellowed from the glow of the ceiling display, but they looked like they'd been carved from old walrus tusks and were long and curved inward. *The better for tearing* I thought with a cringe.

I kept my chant rolling off my tongue in the quiet lilt my father had instilled in me when doing my magical charms. He said the *Green Mother* always enjoyed the Irish brogue.

Prescott didn't make a move toward me while I chanted the incantation that passed on the air between us like a boat on the sea. I stood rooted in place, bathed in the eerie yellow light from the constellations dangling above us. I stared into his inflamed eyes while I softly spoke the words, slowing my breathing to conserve my energy for a prolonged warding. At the conclusion of the chanting, he seemed to be mesmerized, a theory I tested by inching toward the doorway. He didn't react so I chanced another two inches, shuffling my feet as quietly as possible on the dark wooden floor.

Prescott stared ahead to the place I once occupied, allowing me to slip around him and out of the room without his notice. I ran down the stairs to the first floor and out the front door which was still slightly open. I got to my car and as I jumped into it I heard a terrible, throaty howl coming from the house. Prescott must have come out of his trance and found me gone. I fumbled while inserting the key, still unfamiliar with my new car, but when the engine fired up I swung into a wide arc and raced away from the house ignoring the fact that I almost slid side-ways out of the drive   I didn't have to stick around to figure out that Prescott wasn't going to be a gentleman and answer any questions regarding the beasts from the basement. He WAS one for heaven's sake! Now, I had to consider how to tell Jason and Morgan about Prescott's transformation from man to werewolf without sounding like some lunatic who'd over-dosed on late night movies!

As I drove at a frightfully slow pace over the icy roads back to Iron Mountain I had time to consider what I had just seen. The dark pool of liquid on the floor of Prescott's kitchen didn't seem as innocent now. It had to be blood. *But whose blood* I asked myself. I hadn't gotten to the other rooms and wondered if there was a victim somewhere in the house. My father always said my curiosity was like a wild horse with lots of instincts and energy, but like that horse, tore off in many a wrong direction without a strong guiding hand on the reins. The only person I knew up here who could help keep me focused was Jason Tate and he didn't even know I was up here. I felt very alone, and very sure I wasn't.

The road was still dark and even more treacherous as there was a wet snow falling and the temperature had noticeably dropped. I approached each curve with caution, knowing if I slipped off the road up here, I might never be found in the dense forests surrounding me. As I slowed to negotiate another twist and turn in the road I saw something in my side view mirror. My whole body was on heightened alert now as I knew that I wasn't the only being moving in the shadows cast by the surrounding woods.

It was running fast and closing on me because I had slowed to a crawl. Its long snout and massive head would have been frightening to anyone in the light of day, but here, in the bleakness of the dark forest, it was terrifying! I tore my eyes off it for the few minutes I needed to avoid driving off the roadway, and when I looked back I saw a most startling sight. The beast had a pair of eyeglasses hanging from a tufted ear. Prescott had been wearing glasses when I saw him standing in that upstairs room. I snatched quick looks back to the snowy road ahead and saw I was descending into the valley where Iron Mountain sat like a finish line in this race I had to win.

When I turned onto the highway, I was able to increase my speed. The beast gradually fell back, but I was still able to see it clearly enough to detect changes to its form. It was now slowing to a stop and so did I, now that I felt secure enough to watch it from the safety of this town road. The glasses that had been snagged in its fur had slipped off into the snow as it seemed to be shifting in shape. While I watched, the fur and hide of the creature began to slough away. He crouched down so his nakedness was concealed by the shadows and some deep snow drifts. I could see his chest and face clearly now. It was Malcom Prescott and he had deep lacerations all over his torso and face. I guessed the rest of him was likely cut to ribbons as well, but dare not leave the safety of my car to see. His injuries might explain that dark puddle in his kitchen. The cold might have helped staunch any bleeding, but he must have already lost a lot of blood.

Prescott was on his knees now, and appeared to be looking around as if he wasn't sure where he was or how he'd gotten there. I felt a moment of alarm as it dawned on me that he probably would die out here in the cold if he wasn't helped. But how could I approach a man who'd been a nightmarish creature a few moments ago. One who would certainly have torn me apart if I hadn't made good my escape.

Just as I weighed the consequences of aiding this strange man-beast, I saw something large and fast-moving crossing the white expanse, lit by the high moon and coming directly toward Prescott. I thought it was a timber wolf, known to roam these deep forests. Perhaps he was drawn here by the scent of Prescott's bloody torso. As it drew near I saw clearly the shaggy form of an outlandishly large, reddish-brown wolf. It stopped just short of the kneeling Prescott and after circling the still figure once, he lunged in a blur of movement and Prescott disappeared into the snow. There was no scream, no cry for help, just a spine chilling primordial growl penetrating the pristine quiet of the glacial air. The *Green Mother* surely moaned with the savagery of it. The sound of bones snapping like kindling carried in the dead silence, and I cringed.

I sat for several minutes, watching like a phantom behind my fogged windows. After what seemed an eternity of listening in helpless terror to the low crunch and growls, the wolf padded off toward the shadowy woods, stopping for a moment to lick at the red gore covering its muzzle. It looked back over its hunched, massive shoulders and I felt its eyes peering through the dark interior of my car. When it lopped off into the thick screen of the trees, I knew it had destroyed whatever Prescott had become. My heart was still thudding in my chest as I realized what I had witnessed and now I was certain the red wolf had not just happened upon Prescott. I knew in my heart I was followed up here and "Big Red" was more than an enormous wolf. Somehow, he was my self-appointed champion. I felt something inside me twitch with that realization. I didn't know if I should be glad or afraid.

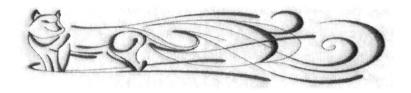

Chapter 19

It was a few minutes before I snapped back into reality and began my cautious decent into Iron Mountain's city square. I was shaking and had a death grip on the steering wheel as I finally made it to the city limits. Being a magic user didn't shield me from being scared out of my long johns, it just gave me a fighting chance over an opponent. My experience to this point was limited to helping my dad round up and subdue some rogue garden fairies that had been turning farm animals into shambling giant sloths for fun. (But that's another story.) Werewolves, monster dogs and giant timber wolves were another kind of nightmare altogether.

As I half expected, there was a light on at the "Ugly Baker's" in spite of the late hour. By now, it was nearly 11:00 and I suspected Gus was getting ready for the morning baking. The snow blurred the streets and pasted itself on the cold windows of the store fronts. Only the bakery seemed to hold any life within.

I decided not to go inside just yet. *Gus has better things to do than to listen to my ravings*, I thought glumly. I was pretty sure I wasn't ready to tell him what I'd seen, either. This was really a problem for the law. I cruised by the shops and headed over to the Sheriff's office praying silently that Jason and not Leo was on duty.

The jail and Jason's squad car came into view as my overworked wipers cleared my windshield of the heavy, persistent snow. I parked as close to the front door as possible and when I got out, my legs felt new to the art of walking upright. I was calmer now, but my body hadn't caught on to the idea that I was safe. I opened the door and spotted Jason hunched over a stack of files on his desk. Looking up at the blast of frigid air, he jumped from his chair and came toward me.

"Cathleen, what on earth took you out in this weather? Is everything alright at your place?" I stepped past him and slumped down in the chair by his desk and after removing my hat and gloves I began.

"Jason, what I have to tell you will sound so bizarre that you'll probably think I've lost my mind, but I swear to you, I am sober and sane."

"Whatever it is, Cathleen, I think I know you well enough to know you are always sober and sane. Let's hear it." He took a seat behind his desk and stared intently at me as I began.

With the telling of my tale, I felt even more unnerved just reliving it. After an aggressive and probing interrogation in which he demanded to know how I had overcome Prescott, exhausted, I finally told Jason about the magic spell I had chanted. Jason relaxed and nodded as if he used Celtic mantras all the time in his police work.

He was unhappy that I'd gone up the mountain to do my own questioning, but he'd suspected my motives for going home earlier from the station and wasn't all that surprised. "You really find it hard to take orders don't you Magic Lady?"

I studied him closely and answered "Guess I might. But I think you'll understand if I ask that you keep my methods of investigation between us."

He said "Naturally." And that was that.

He then sat behind his desk and didn't speak or ask any questions for what felt like an eternity. I could hear the wind picking up and a quick glance out the window showed my car disappearing like another act of magic under the white blanket of snow being thrown over it.

Jason finally moved from his chair to the window and with his back to me, in a subdued voice he said, "It's time you heard the legend of The Wolf Master of Iron Mountain, Cathleen. At least, we like to call it a legend. Seems the events of the past few days go a long way to dispelling any wishful notions of fairy tales regarding this place." With that said, he sighed deeply like a broken man and sat back down behind his desk. The small lamp next to his right arm cast a kaleidoscope of shadows on his face and I sensed that I was about to hear a story of loss and dark memories.

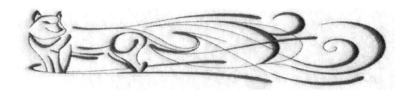

Chapter 20

"By the time I was15," he began, "my parents were already dead and I had a younger brother to look after. Jeff was a good kid, funny, smart, full of mischief like any 13 year old. He loved the woods around here and would go hunting squirrel, rabbit, anything that he knew I'd fix him for supper." Jason was smiling at the memories he was conjuring up, but that sly grin began to fade as he continued. "When the tourists started to disappear from the trails around Iron Mountain, I told Jeff he'd not be doing any more hunting or fishing until they found out why folks were going missing. He bridled at that order from me and one day, when I was working after school, he took off with his shot gun and a sack for the birds he planned on bagging. Neighbors up the way saw him cross the road into the woods with that gear, and said that he was only wearing a light coat, like he wasn't going to be gone long. It was late September and getting chilly in the evenings. When I got home around six expecting him to be stirring the stew I'd made the night before, I found an empty house. That's when I saw his gun was missing from the bedroom." Jason sat quietly for a minute before he continued.

"There were all kinds of wild theories and rumors being tossed around back then, but one kept resurfacing over the years. It was about an old Navajo Indian who appeared in Iron Mountain back in the mid-1800s. The story goes he was on the run from the law because of a number of mysterious murders around what's now called the "Four Corners" area in the south west. This Indian was reportedly a powerful Shaman, but had been driven out of his clan by the Navajo Chiefs from that region because of his evil powers. Legend goes, he showed up here in Iron Mountain saying he was a trapper like so many others. He stayed in a small cabin near the edge of town, close to where your house is situated. When torn up bodies started to be found around the outskirts of town, suspicion fell on him again.

According to the old newspapers I found in the town Archives, he allegedly took off for the upper mountain ranges where tracking him was pretty much impossible. There were reports over the years of sightings up there by hunters and trappers working the range and some even claimed the old Indian had been living with a pack of unnaturally huge wolves in the abandoned, Iron Mountain Coal Mine. He supposedly is still up there, making him around one hundred and thirty years old."

He let that number sink into my already spinning head before he went on. "That mine was considered a killer pit to the folks around here as it had taken so many of our fathers and sons. Ironically, part of the lure to the tourist coming up here was to find that Indian and discover his secret of longevity. Some believed there was some sort of elixir the old Indian concocted down in the mine shaft that might be related to the giant wolves. Others said it was something in the mine itself, maybe a rare fungus he had discovered and was using in his elixir. In any case, they came with hope and ignorance of the mountains and over the next 30 odd years they perished in the snows, or just vanished off the mountain trails and from the cabins they rented from the locals.

Twenty years ago the town council for Iron Mountain decided the bad press they were getting over all the disappearances had to be dealt with so they hired a couple of mountain boys, hunters with reputations for tracking anything living and surviving in the wild mountain terrain. They thought these men could look for wolf sign around the old mine and track them back to wherever they were holed up and destroy the pack. They left the town hall after taking photos of the expedition and the two would-be heroes for the *Iron Mountain News*. They were fully equipped for the wilderness and packing enough fire power for a small army when they waived the victory sign and left. They haven't been seen since."

I began to stir in my chair and slipped out of my coat. It had been a long and riveting story, but I had a question that needed an answer before I could get into this any deeper. "Jason" I said in a subdued voice, "do you believe my story about Prescott turning into a wolf creature?"

He looked at me for a long moment before answering simply, "Yes. That animal I killed in the station was beginning to change back into human form as it was dying. The first one had already lost the fur on its front and I didn't see that until I turned it over after you'd left.

"Do you feel any guilt over killing them Jason? They were men once."

He stared at me with one, cold green eye. "They lost their right to humane treatment when they gave their spirits to that Shaman, Cathleen. I haven't told anyone else and I don't know if I ever will get a chance, but I recognized one of those beasts when he started to change. He was one of the people we thought lost on the mountain. I was part of the search party looking for him when he went missing 11 years ago. I helped the old Sheriff put together a pose and led it up into the area around the old mine." He paused for a moment and glanced at a tack board covered with photos of missing persons.

Then he continued, "This man was employed by a large pharmaceutical company to hunt down the Shaman so they could discover his secret of longevity. He had a reputation as a big game hunter and strutted around town like a peacock with all his fancy gear. I had words with him before he left and warned him that no one would be able to help him if he got into trouble up there. I'll never forget his laughing in my face and saying, "A mountain is just a big pile of rocks." Well, he never came down from the mountain and that big company didn't get to make its fortune selling forever-life pills to the world."

We continued discussing the disappearances and whether the missing were victims or participants for several minutes, often raising our voices to counter the storm which seemed to have gathered some serious winds while we were talking. I tried to look out the window again to check that my car hadn't blown down the street, but I could barely see out now as the snow covered the window like thick gauze. I turned back to Jason and saw him studying my face. "Cathleen, I need to confide in you, but maybe you have already guessed my biggest fear."

"I think you're afraid that the next beast you have to kill may be your brother," I said softly.

Jason looked down at his hands, folded on top of his desk. "Yes, I am. But that won't stop me from doing my job." He took a deep breath and looking up at me said firmly, "If he's one of them, he has to be destroyed."

I nodded my head to show my support for what would be an amazingly unselfish act. Jason stood up and moved around the desk to where I sat.

He leaned down and took my hands in his and spoke in an intimate voice, "Whatever happens, I said I wouldn't let anything happen to you and I meant it, Cathleen. In the short time we've known each other, I feel strangely attached to you, like I've known you my whole life and I won't let you get hurt. I promise."

I looked back at him and smiling said, "Thank you, Jason. I know how you feel because we do seem to be pretty comfortable in one another's company. You didn't even blink when I told you I'm a magic user. It's as if you've had some experience with people like me."

A tight smile flickered across his face, and he said, "I always felt there was something different about you, just by the way I felt around you. And I doubt there's *anyone* quite like you, Cathleen, but right now, I can use all the help I can muster if I'm going to survive whatever devils await me up there. Giving my hand a quick squeeze, he went back to sit behind his desk again and we were both quiet, listening to the wail of the storm as it tore through the night.

After a moment of reflection on the question of Jason's comfort level around Magic I asked, "Have you ever known any Magic users, Jason?"

He looked thoughtful, like he was trying to decide whether or not to answer my question, then replied, "When I was around seven, I started to have what I came to think of as "waking dreams." They scared the heck out of me because I knew when things were going to happen. I knew when the postman would be bringing a special letter, or if someone in the family would be getting hurt or sick. I hated these little sights into the future and was sure I'd be punished when I died if I kept having them. I came from people who believed in retribution for evil doers and these waking dreams seemed very bad to my seven year old head.

The visions kept up until I was around ten and had a strong vision. I had gone up to the coal mine to meet my dad as his shift had ended. I'd often meet him as he was coming home because I couldn't wait to tell him of my day. When I got to the coal mine road I saw men streaming down it, carrying lunch buckets and helmets, but they didn't look right to me. They weren't speaking or joking with one another and they had a grey look about them that I thought was just coal dust covering their faces and clothes. I stopped walking and let them pass as I watched and that's when I knew…they were all dead. Before I could see my dad, I forced myself to snap out of the vision, but I guess I already knew he'd be like all these other miners had been. I just didn't know when it would happen."

I said, "Jason, what an awful experience for you, but did you keep it to yourself or tell anyone?"

"I decided I had to tell my mom. I'll never forget the look on her face. She was terrified." Jason stopped speaking for a moment to try and collect himself from what was clearly an emotional experience. He inhaled deeply and continued.

"She tried to comfort me when I told her about what I'd seen and my other special insights to the future, even though I could see how concerned she was. There was no mistaking the fact that she felt they were *not* something I should encourage when I started to have one. She warned that I was never to tell anyone about them and was about to leave my room when I asked her to explain what was happening to me. Reluctantly, she told me about an aunt I never heard of before, her sister, Margaret Ann.

She had been able to "see" things in the future too and used to do "readings" for folks around town back then to earn a few dollars. Margaret Ann never read for anyone she felt she knew well, like a friend, but I guess she was dead-right with strangers who came to her. The word quickly got around because people were pretty desperate around these parts and soon lots of folks heard about her extraordinary abilities. Perfect strangers started coming from surrounding towns, sometimes hiking a whole day to get to my grandparents house, seeking out Margaret Ann for a look into their futures. She never turned these folks away because they were so grateful for her visions and she never charged those people who came in innocence and fear, but couldn't pay the quarter.

Mom told me Margaret Ann was pretty much ostracized from her family after a year of this open "charlatanism" and "devil's work" as locals and their preacher called it, even the ones that had already had her read for them. They began saying she was a White Witch. That's what they called her, but I think they were all scared to death of her and what they couldn't understand. This is a small town and always has been. Being different was not something you wanted to advertise."

When he stopped talking I jumped in with a question. "What happened to Margaret Ann?"

"She left Iron Mountain right before she turned nineteen, about a year after they made her stop looking where she shouldn't be looking." He seemed lost in his thoughts and said, "Mom had told me that Margaret Ann was gifted, but that Iron Mountain was no place for her special talents. People here were frightened of her and didn't like it that she could see into their lives. Mom told me my aunt just disappeared off the mountain one day, like the mist off Iron Lake, but I suspected there was more to it than that. Guess even as a kid of ten, I had a deep curiosity about unsolved mysteries." He gave a quick smile to me.

I wrapped my arms around myself. Jason knew I had more questions, but I wanted to allow him a second to come back from his unsettling childhood memories first.

I sat silently, mulling over all Jason had just shared about his family. I wondered if he was still afraid of unusual abilities in himself or others, to mentally touch the life force in people. I looked over at him as he peered closely at his clasped hands as if looking for some hidden clues about himself. The storm shook the building as it pushed against its walls as if trying to tear it down around us.

But one question just couldn't be left unasked. "Jason, do you still have your visions of the future?

He looked over at me.

"Are you wondering if I'd do a reading for you? He smiled weakly.

"No, of course not, but do you still see future events?"

"Not events. I haven't for many years," he answered. "I do seem to have very strong instincts about people. I pick up on small things that mostly go unnoticed, like the way someone's eyes shift or go out of focus. Very helpful in my line of work." He grinned over at me and went on. "And I guess my curiosity about what's happening around me leads me to do some heavy-duty thinking about events past and present, trying to understand them and find the truth in the story.

I'm actually something of a history buff, by the way. I learned plenty from our town's archives about the *unexplained* in and around Iron Mountain. When I started searching through them a number of years ago, I found reports of werewolves dating back to the late 1700s in some of the Indian folklore from this region's native tribes. There were also sightings recorded as late as the time of the disappearances from Iron Mountain. I've read all I can get my hands on regarding the Dark Magic reportedly used by some Shamans that give them incredible powers. I try to keep an open mind to the mysteries in life. You could say and I've come to think of Magic as a device for good as well as evil."

Stopping for a moment he said, "Cathleen, I honestly don't think there is anything about you that will scare me off in case that's what you're thinking."

That was *exactly* what I was thinking! I was hoping too, he wouldn't be telling me about any future events that might involve long snouts with lots of teeth. I prefer discovering my own demons and didn't want the burden of knowing them in advance!

He kept smiling at me with his crooked grin, and I knew some of our investigation would be of a personal nature. The little shiver I felt wasn't from the cold this time.

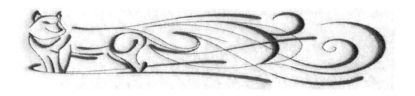

Chapter 21

Jason and I had moved into the small kitchen off the squad room to brew some much needed coffee. "We better stay alert, Cathleen," he was saying while we got out the mugs and cream. "By the way, I had the bodies of those two basement creatures taken to the local crematorium and had them burned. I didn't allow the funeral home owner to view them, just said they were drifters and that I'd pay the costs. If he had any questions, he kept them to himself."

I wrapped my hands around the steaming cup he handed me and felt the chill that had started to creep into my body begin to recede. But there was something I hadn't shared and I thought it was time I did.

"Jason," I said after a sip, "I think I was followed up the mountain to Prescott's house."

"What makes you say that," he asked with a serious expression on his face. The patch over his left eye seemed to age him and I realized how tired he must be as he should have left here hours ago for his home and bed.

I took a breath. "When I got to Prescott's house I thought I saw something moving in the woods close to where I parked my car. It ran off and I didn't see it clearly, but I thought it was some kind of animal. Later, when Prescott was chasing me down the mountain and he stopped and started to change back, that huge reddish-brown wolf came out of the woods and, well, you know the rest."

"Did you feel threatened by the wolf that attacked Prescott?" he asked.

"Actually, I had the strangest feeling that he had followed me up there and meant to protect me as odd as that sounds even to me. And the weirdest thing of all was the wolf seemed *familiar* somehow."

Jason sat for a minute digesting this theory and then said, "If that's true, Cathleen, it means someone's walking around Iron Mountain right now who's one of these monsters. It means they can change form at will and stalk a particular person. They are able to act on their human motivation or intent in their animal form."

I hadn't considered that particular point until he made me face the truth. If Big Red actually was a self-appointed guardian to me, he had to have made a conscious decision not to add me to his lunch menu. Now I was wondering just how many of these shaggy carnivores were roaming free from detection and were somewhat less threatening to people? I didn't have an answer, but I secretly hoped that "Big Red" as I'd come to think of him would have my back if I needed serious protecting. I didn't voice this hope to Jason, as he seemed convinced that they were all monsters and must be killed.

Jason, starting on his second cup of coffee, began to pace again. He talked in low tones almost as if he didn't want the storm raging outside to catch his words and blow them to a lurking beast. Looking down at me he seemed to be searching for a way to ask his next question. "Cathleen, have you ever heard of Skin Walkers?"

Actually, I had come across references to them a few times in my life. I answered, "When I studied Native American Cultures for a course in Anthropology they were part of the folklore of some indigenous cultures. I know the Navajo Indians among others believe there were some among them who could change shape and form and become animals, or other creatures with fantastic strength and mystical powers."

"Yes," he said, "and I don't want you to think I've started to lose my grip, but I suspect we are dealing with a Medicine man or Shaman, with those kinds of dark powers. An actual Skin Walker."

I felt my eyes go wide with horror. "Jason, you can't be serious! It's the 21st century. That was a legend from primitive cultures, centuries ago."

Jason just looked back at me with a quirky grin and said, "This from the woman who uses Celtic Magic! Besides, that legend has been around for hundreds of years and with all the crazy stuff happening here in Iron Mountain, I'm not going to be too quick to dismiss it."

For the sake of argument I said, "OK. Let's just say we're dealing with a Skin Walker. Is he, or it, in control of the werewolves and monster dogs we've seen?"

Jason stopped pacing. "I believe he's their pack leader. There can be no other explanation. He's attacked these people and changed them to form a pack of killers. He uses them to capture and change others to keep his pack strong."

I asked, "Do you think the red wolf was part of his pack?"

"No," he said, "or if he was, he was able to control his transformations and once he could do that, he was able to choose for himself who he'd attack."

I thought about this a moment and said, "What about the Indian Shaman, the Skin Walker? Wouldn't he try to kill Big Red?"

Jason gave me a quick smile at the name I had dubbed my would-be rescuer.

"Probably, if he could come down from the mountain, but I don't think he can leave the shelter of his lair, which I now suspect is in the old Iron Mountain Coal Mine."

I looked at him questioningly. "It sounds like you think Big Red is down here, Jason, in the town."

"From what you've told me about Big Red, he seems able to make choices and that means he's not totally in the control of the Shaman. And yes, I think he may be hiding in plain sight, Cathleen. Right here in Iron Mountain." I gave a little shudder because even though I was sure Big Red was not going to hurt me, I didn't know his intentions toward other unsuspecting town folk.

Jason was scrapping the frost that had formed from the condensation on his office window so he could take a look at the bleak scene outside. The storm had almost become a howling, living thing outside this small outpost of safety. Swirling snow was being driven by the heavy winds into every crack and crevice of the building. My car was obliterated and only a large lump sitting under the wavering street light signified its existence. Jason turned his green eye to me and said, "You aren't going anywhere tonight, Cathleen. This storm is a killer. I can make up one of the cots in a cell for you if you won't mind sleeping in a jail house for one night."

I tried to demure, but he wouldn't hear of my trying to find my way home. Actually, I was secretly very relieved as I was still pretty jangled and I felt much safer in Jason's company. I didn't hold out much hope of sleeping, but said I'd try to rest. With that I curled up under a scratchy wool blanket and closed my eyes. Only Jason's desk lamp illuminated the office as he sat back down behind his desk again, lost in thought. The cell area off the main room where I lay curled into a tight ball was in heavy shadows.

Shouting. Who was shouting? Where was I? I sat up and realized I was in the jail cell. I must have dozed off because I was jerked back to consciousness by the sound of that shouting voice.

"I'm reporting for duty, Sheriff!" It was the Deputy riding a cyclone of swirling snow into the office. The wind nearly ripped the door out of his hand as he struggled to slam it shut against the fury of the storm.

"Leo!" Jason shouted in disbelief as he sprang to his feet. "I thought I told you not to worry about taking a shift tonight. It's a dangerous storm and you risked getting lost in these conditions man!"

"Aw, Jason," Leo said, while stomping his heavy snow-covered boots. "You know I have the direction sense of a hound dog. And besides I didn't want you to be by your lonesome out here. I figured you could use some of Gus's fresh doughnuts too." He held up a gloved hand to brandish a bag from the Ugly Baker's.

He hadn't seen me in the dark cell. I came out in my stocking feet. Leo didn't hear my approach and nearly jumped a foot into the air when he saw me standing there. I thought the light was playing tricks on me because I saw his eyes turn yellow and then quickly fade back to their normal dark brown. His wild red hair was partially crammed under his official knit police cap and the buttons on his coat were in the wrong holes making the jacket hang strangely on his lean figure.

"Hey, Leo!" I said with a smile that I hoped would calm his fright.

"Miss Cathleen! What on earth are you doing here? Was that your car under all that snow out there?"

He was smiling at me, but I noticed it never reached his eyes which were nervously darting around the room as if searching for a way out. Strange vibes were rolling off him. He shot Jason a dark look, and it dawned on me that he seemed almost jealous. I wondered if Jason had picked up some negative emotion coming from his deputy. From what I knew of Leo from recent conversations and comments made by Jason, I understood that he was a long-time bachelor that had an idealized "dream girl" in mind for wife material.

I remembered something about red hair, and squirmed a bit as he seemed to be studying me under the harsh florescent lights. I smoothed down my sleep rumpled auburn hair self consciously.

"Yes, at least it was my car. Probably more of a snowbank by now," I responded in a friendly tone. "I came in earlier to speak with the Sheriff and got stuck here. I was resting in the cell when I heard you come in."

"Cathleen was stopping by to check on the station situation and the storm got too strong to send her out in it again," Jason added.

"Sure," Leo said, grinning, "no sense in risking life and limb just to sleep in your own bed when there's a perfectly clean cell cot to be had." I noticed how the smile he gave us was forced and never reached his dark eyes.

Jason and I exchanged a quick look and then laughed briefly at Leo's attempt at humor.

"Leo," I said smoothly, "How are the roads out there?"

He answered, "Let's just say I'm glad we have these doughnuts and some coffee on the brew. I wouldn't relish going back out in the dark and it's a general white-out condition all over the mountain according to Gus. Hey, Jason," he said, turning his attention back to the Sheriff, "what did you end up doing with those bodies anyway?"

"I had them cremated, Leo. Best thing to do with them. By the way, I was hoping you'd be there to help me get them loaded into the mortuary van."

"Oh, sorry Sheriff," Leo answered. "I had to get back to the bakery to do some heavy lifting for Gus." He had moved off into the kitchen to get his own mug of coffee and deposit the donuts. Jason and I stood in the doorway watching him while he filled his cup.

It seemed odd to me that Leo would put pastry making over disposal of the creatures from the station basement. Evidently,

Jason had a similar thought as he gave Leo a quizzical look and then shrugged and turned to go back to his desk.

Leo stood silently holding his coffee. He reached up to stuff his knit hat into a pocket, immediately releasing his wiry red mop and walked back into the front office where Jason and I had resumed our seats and conversation in low tones. We weren't ignoring him, but I knew Jason had to test the waters his Deputy was swimming in.

Shuffling from foot to foot nervously, he walked over to the window and after scraping a small peep hole with his thumb nail, began to pensively gaze out. He didn't acknowledge either of us when we began talking about the monsters we'd already found, but when Jason purposely mentioned the words " Skin Walker" he spun around so quickly some of his hot drink sloshed over the rim of his cup.

The look on his face was frightening before he was able to get control of himself. He tried to cover up his alarm by yelping over the hot liquid and fussing over the wet spot on the floor. Jason and I glanced side-long at one another and I saw a fleeting look of alarm on his face. I had seen him place his side arm into his desk drawer earlier and now he carefully moved his hand in that direction. I jumped up and rushed over to Leo, helping him wipe the mess up with tissues off Jason's desk. This helped to distract him while Jason slid the drawer open and retrieved his gun.

Leo said in a subdued voice, "Well, I've never been known for my graceful nature, right Sheriff?"

Jason smiled tightly and said, "Not exactly, Leo. By the way, what did you say you were helping Gus with earlier this evening?"

Leo shot him a quick look while getting back on his feet. "Well, just some heavy flour sacks and such. Gus is real strong for a little guy, but those sacks are like cement bags for him to lift."

"Strange," Jason said, "that there was a delivery that late in the day though."

"Yeah, but the driver said the weather delayed him," Leo responded in his unhurried sort of way. While this conversation took place I had moved closer to the front door pretending to peer out the frosted window. I knew that if our suspicions were correct, Jason and I could be in deadly danger.

Leo had returned to the small kitchen and was refilling his mug when Jason stood up. He had his hand down by his side where his service pistol was held tightly against his leg. "So, Leo," he said, with an edge of threat in his voice, "I think there might be something you need to tell me. Want to start with why you followed Cathleen up the mountain earlier tonight?"

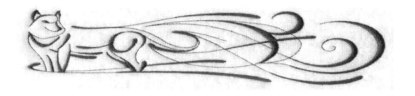

Chapter 22

Leo didn't seem to hear Jason as he went on refilling the mug. He came back to the office and stood in front of Jason's desk. "What crazy kind of question is that, Jason? I was with you most of the afternoon."

Jason looked steadily back at him and said, "I'm talking about after you left for what I thought was only a dinner break."

I spoke up. "Leo, you came by my house to check on me and said Jason asked you to do that."

"The Sheriff didn't exactly ask me, Miss Cathleen. I just figured I'd do it as I knew he was concerned about you."

Jason said, "Leo, please answer my question. Why did you follow Cathleen earlier this evening?"

Leo slumped down into the chair in front of the desk. He suddenly looked as deflated as a week-old balloon. "Sheriff," he said, barely opening his mouth to speak. "There are some things better left unsaid and undiscovered." His eyes were downcast as if he was looking for his words in the steam rising from his cup. "I knew Miss Cathleen wasn't really going out to run errands like she claimed, so I decided to follow her to make sure she wouldn't get into any trouble up there on the mountain."

"What kind of trouble, Leo? I was only going to meet with Prescott." I asked this in the calmest voice I could manage.

"There are things about these mountains around here that even the Sheriff couldn't fathom. And he's a pretty good mountain man himself." Leo had said this looking directly at

Jason who still stood with his gun against his thigh. He was obviously uneasy while he searched Leo's face for the truth. Leo looked at me intently and added, "Besides, Prescott wasn't the man you thought he was. He was dangerous and could have hurt you...or worse." Jason slid his gun back into his holster and sat behind his desk.

"Leo, you know he's dead don't you? Prescott?" Leo looked up and replied, "Guess you already know the answer to that question, Jason." With that he got up and started for the door where I stood.

Jason jumped out of his seat and said, "Hold on, Leo! I think you're in a world of trouble and I want to help you. Tell me about the Indian Skin Walker and Cathleen and I will do my best to get you free of him. We can fight him together."

Leo gave a snort like a laugh that got choked off. "Jason," he said staring with the eyes of a man who knew too much "my only way out from that world is by traveling in a wooden coffin." With that, he looked sadly into my eyes for a moment and pushed past me into the white maze that was Iron Mountain.

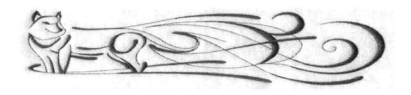

Chapter 23

I turned to Jason and asked, "What are we going to do now?"

Jason looked out the window behind his desk. He couldn't see more than a few feet before the window frosted over again. I was beginning to shiver with the cold that seeped through the walls and floor.

Jason must have seen me rubbing my arms and said rather distractedly, "Sorry, Cathleen. You must be getting cold. I'll crank up the heat and see if that helps warm us up a bit."

I felt he was trying to avoid answering me. "What about my question?"

He turned from the thermostat and in a voice full of doubt and unhappiness he said, "Wish I knew. I can't exactly arrest him on our suspicions alone. We need to know what he knows and what he's going to do about us guessing his secret." It made sense to get Leo to unravel the knotty questions swirling around the disappearances and the Indian Shaman we suspected was behind them. I had an idea that came to me as I watched Jason unlock his gun rack and retrieve two shotguns and a box of ammo.

"Jason," I said, "I think I know a way to get Leo to help us discover the whereabouts of the Shaman."

Jason laid the rifles down across the desk top and gave me his full attention. "We need to set the right bait and get him to follow it up the mountain again."

"Oh, no! You are NOT going back up there, Cathleen! You skated last time, but there's no way you can be that lucky twice, not with that Skin Walker on the prowl."

I looked at him a long time before I responded. "Jason, I know that Leo will follow me again. He has some sort of protective instinct toward me, or even some kind of infatuation. I think he interpreted my friendliness as interest on my part. I've noticed how he looks at me with a far-off dreamy expression. It made me a bit uncomfortable at first, and even Gus noticed it. He keeps him busy whenever I come into the bakery so we can visit without an audience.

I think more importantly though, is the fact that he didn't attack me when I was at Prescott's house; he had ample opportunity. He could have torn me apart like he did Prescott, but that wasn't what he wanted. That's not why he followed me up there. He really meant to protect me and I believe he will again if I go back."

"Exactly how would you get back up there with the roads probably impassable by now?" he asked with a dark look on his face.

"I was hoping you'd drive me in that tank you call a squad car," I said. "We could cruise by the bakery to be sure Leo saw us leaving and then make our way back to where I last saw Prescott. If we need to get away quickly, that road leads directly back here."

He didn't seem happy with my plan, but looking at me closely asked, "What do you hope to accomplish by putting us in certain danger?"

"We can find out where this evil Shaman has made his lair and then destroy him!" I said with more enthusiasm than I actually felt.

"Don't be naïve, Cathleen. This guy is seriously scary and very powerful if he can do half of what I suspect he's been doing." He turned away from me and began loading the guns.

I began to mentally calculate our odds with a quick inventory of magic charms and spells I might need to call upon to protect us. Satisfied that I was strong enough to face down the Shaman I said "Jason, you have to trust me in this; I have my own magical powers and I know I am the Shaman's match! Anyway, think about it. Leo is the *only* lead we have to the Skin Walker. We have to do everything we can to see to it that he can't hurt or change any more innocent people... people like your brother."

I knew I wasn't exactly playing fair, but I felt like our opportunity was slipping away. He stopped loading the guns and gave me a hurt look. "Jason," I continued, placing my hand on his arm, "you know we will never be safe here in Iron Mountain until we wipe out the Skin Walker and all of his pack."

Jason's hand hung suspended over the ammo box and I knew I had him.

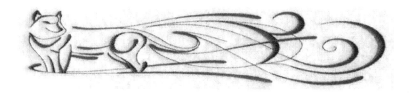

Chapter 24

After twenty minutes of digging his squad car from under a snow mound, we packed the back seat with extra blankets, two heavy duty flashlights with extra batteries and the two shotguns and boxes of ammo. We kept it running to warm it up. It felt like we were going on an Arctic Expedition, but I knew that our plan was every bit as dangerous.

Jason seemed calmer now that we were working with a plan. He stowed the last of our gear which included two pairs of snow shoes that he unearthed from his storage room. I didn't think we'd need them, but then, I didn't think I'd ever be chased down a mountain by a werewolf!

On the way over to the Ugly Baker's, I thought I'd mention something to Jason that seemed pertinent to our plans to survive this trip. "Jason," I said, "my dad was a hunter and a crack shot. He gave me my first shot gun when I was 10. He'd done the gunsmith work on it himself so I could handle it easily. I was actually considered a pretty good shot myself at the gun club I belonged to in Pittsburgh." Jason gave me a sidelong glance as he angled into a snow bank that might have been the street in front of the bakery.

"Can you handle the guns I packed?" he asked.

"Definitely."

"Good," he replied briskly as he opened his door into a strong blast of wind and blinding snow.

We stomped into the warmth of the sweet smelling shop and saw Gus Flores on his chair feeding what would be sweet rolls into the hungry mouth of the oven. "You two never cease to amaze me! He said loudly. There's a blizzard ragging out there in case you hadn't noticed and here you are, in the wee hours of the morning looking for fresh doughnuts."

He chuckled into his long white beard and that's when I noticed something about Gus that seemed out of place. He was wearing heavy woolen pants under his apron. I only saw this because the apron was flapping around his feet and not snug up around his middle as he usually had it secured. It was very warm in the shop and standing in front of the ovens it had to be even hotter. I'd never seen Gus dressed in such heavy clothes when he was actually baking. It was almost as if he had been out in the storm shortly before we arrived.

When he stepped down from his perch, I saw a puddle of water had formed on the chair where he'd stood. My eyes travelled down to his feet and I saw the rugged custom made boots he wore around town. *But not inside while baking*, I thought.

Jason wandered over to the case and leaned on the top. "Gus," he said, "I'm taking Cathleen up the mountain to find Prescott. She saw him earlier and he seemed disoriented. We're concerned that he's taken off into this storm and might need help. If you see Leo, tell him to man the office for me until I get back."

I was trying to look concerned for Gus's sake when he said, "I sure wish you two would reconsider going out into this weather for that creep, Prescott, Sheriff. He wasn't exactly the kind of guy who'd help you out unless there was something in it for him."

"Never-the-less, Gus," Jason answered firmly, "it's my job to safeguard the folks around here. Just be sure Leo gets my message." With that we both turned and went back into the biting cold of the storm.

As Jason and I reentered his warming squad car, I saw a reddish blur of motion coming from behind the bakery and going toward the back door. "Jason, I said quietly as if it might hear, "I think I just saw "Big Red" behind the shop."

"Game on," was all he said.

We turned down the road I had used out of town earlier, listening to the beat of the wipers as they struggled to sweep up the ever-falling snow. When I finally broke the silence, I asked Jason why Big Red was hanging around the bakery if he knew we suspected him of being a werewolf. Jason had a tight grip on the wheel and he seemed to be pushing his heavy vehicle through several feet of snow. After a long pause he answered.

"Cathleen, did you notice how Gus was dressed? " I answered yes and he continued. "Gus and Leo are pretty close and now I'm wondering if we have two of the Skin Walker's changelings in our town living in plain sight."

It was quiet in the SUV for several minutes, except for the swoosh of the wipers and the crunching of the snow as we plowed through the drifts that obscured the roadway. I figured Jason was navigating from memory as there were no real landmarks. After a while I asked, "Jason, are you suggesting that *both* Gus and Leo are werewolves?"

He glanced over at me and said with a small grin, "You can be pretty direct can't you? But to answer that question, yes. I think we are dealing with two of the Shaman's pack and I believe they know that we know. That's going to put a new spin on things now. We sure can't call on Leo for back-up!"

I thought about that for a moment before saying "I think you're wrong about that Jason. I have a strong feeling that Leo will be on our side. And as for Gus, I can't see him doing us any harm as long as he can help it."

"I hope your instincts are right, Cathleen," he said. "We don't know how many of the missing folks will turn up in the wolf pack, but we have to face the fact that we're likely outnumbered."

All conversation stopped as we both seemed lost in our own thoughts. I sat watching the storm tear into the mountain landscape like a blinded beast. The scene brought back memories of another kind of obliteration done to the *Green Mother's* treasured woods.

My parents had taken me up into a grove of sacred trees where they often spent time communing with the *Green Mother*. Now, it was my turn to lend my small voice in her praise. "Molaim thu" "I praise you" in the ancient words of the Druids.

When we had completed our ritual of praise and thanksgiving, my mother said in the same sweet tones to my father, "It would seem we are being observed my dear."

Without losing his own smile or composure, he said "Oh yes, I am certainly aware of that my darlin' girl. Let us join hands with the wee one and do a bit of a blow to ruffle some feathers."

With that, they brought me to my feet and clasping hands in a circle screamed out *"flubaggin anfa"*. This immediately created a wall of wind that shook every tree to its roots and blew anything less than a ton off into the woods around us. Unfortunately for the "Black Cincher" that followed us into the grove to do its dark mischief, his camouflage of lush colored plumage did not protect it from the blast of pine needles and tree branches that beat it to a black pulpy stain.

Equally unfortunate, however, was that the strength of the wind also flattened the woods around us for a quarter-mile. It took my parents several hours of healing prayers to renew the forests back to the *Mother's* standards. This lesson in over-kill wasn't lost on me, but I was sure my current challenge would take a full arsenal.

After a long half hour of driving over the increasingly treacherous roads, I excitedly pointed out to Jason the last spot I'd seen Prescott. It was at the curve, just before it flattened out

and I recognized a large boulder that seemed suspended in space as it sat in the white landscape.

He stopped his squad car and left it idling as we both went to the rear seat and retrieved the guns. After checking them for a full load and jacking one into the chamber, we were ready to set off up the road to where I thought we'd find Prescott's torn remains.

Because it had been snowing for several hours and blowing gale-force winds up there, there was no immediate evidence of an animal attack. The wind was tearing into our clothing like unseen hands trying to rip them away and expose us to the frigid air so we both crouched down to minimize the impact. Jason took the stock of his gun and started poking into the drifts around the most likely spot while I held one of the flashlights and directed it over the area he was searching. After several attempts he finally hit something hard and swept away some of the thick snow with his gloved hand to reveal a long white bone protruding through a yellowish layer of snow.

"Big Red must have marked this as his kill," Jason said almost as if talking to himself. The bone looked like a long leg bone and when he pulled it free, the attached knee proved it. There were still threads of flesh attached in places, but there were also what looked like gnaw marks up and down what was left of the thigh bone. Jason looked over at me and asked if I was doing ok. He likely believed I'd be pretty squeamish.

"I'm fine, Jason, I said in answer to his inquiring look. " I helped my dad skin and gut animals after we went hunting. Though I don't think I'd like to see more of this kill site."

We left shortly after covering the spot carefully with a tree limb from nearby and tying an old rag on a branch so that we might retrieve the remains when possible. Jason scanned the area and said we'd best keep our shot guns in front with us in case they were needed in a hurry.

With that, we began our drive through the moon-streaked landscape until we came to Prescott's vacant house. At least we hoped it was empty so we might do some reconnoitering for possible clues tying Prescott to the Skin Walker and maybe answering our questions on his whereabouts. We needed to act quickly, before the Shaman got a hint of our mission and sent out his twisted wolf pack to find us. All my senses were on demon alert as we stepped from the car.

The house was silent and even more eerie, as if coiling around itself, ready to spring at us. The front door was now closed, *Maybe the wind blew it shut* I thought, vainly hoping that was true.

"Let's go through the kitchen door, Cathleen." Jason was whispering in my ear. I gave an involuntary shudder, remembering the large inky puddle on the floor. We crept as quietly as possible through the brittle snow crust which sounded like bones shattering under our feet. We reached the back of the house and entered like two cat burglars.

By contrast, it felt like our very breath was amplified in the deathly stillness of the darkened kitchen. The pool of what was assuredly blood shimmered wetly in the weak moonlight creeping into the kitchen from the open doorway.

As we made our way with the aid of our large, Sheriff-size flashlights, I was able to guide our path to the staircase. "I think we should start upstairs, Jason". Since that was where I had seen the changing and demonic looking Prescott, I felt that room held some significance to our search for clues. There was something evil about the hanging planets and the glowing galaxy that tinged the room in mystery.

We slowly made our way up the staircase and stopped at the landing to listen before entering the yellowish glow of the first bedroom.

As we stepped over the threshold Jason switched off his own flashlight so he could better see the universe as we knew it spread out in perfect order above our heads.

"There are many Indian traditions and ceremonies that are based on the movement of the planets and the stars." He spoke in hushed tones and even that seemed too loud to my ears.

I looked around quickly to see if anyone had crept into the room behind us, but saw only the empty doorway and our footprints clearly marking the wooden floor. As I looked down where our feet had left wet streaks across the dark wood, I realized there was a thick covering of dust scattered over the floor's surface. *Funny, I didn't notice that before* I thought to myself. "Jason, there's something different about this room," I said softly.

He looked down at me and I said, "I'm certain this thick dust wasn't here earlier. It couldn't have gotten this way so quickly." He switched his flashlight back on and pointed it downward, sweeping the room with its bright beam. "That's not dust, Cathleen" he said "It looks like ash to me."

"Ashes from …?" I trailed off. He moved to my side and took my arm at the elbow, steering me out of the bedroom and back to the hallway.

"Cathleen," he said in a tight voice, "we need to check the other rooms, but I want to do it as quickly as possible. Do you think you can do that room down the hall if I take this one on my right?"

While I didn't fancy the idea of splitting up, I knew we had to maximize our time here and could only accomplish that by covering more ground. I nodded curtly and turned to investigate the room at the end of the hall. My shotgun was nestled securely by my side and gave me a sense of security that I sorely needed then. I began a *whisper chant* so that I could mask my movements as I made my way over creaky floor boards.

The door to this room was shut tight and I was afraid to speculate what might lie within its steely silence. As I turned the old-fashioned glass knob, I realized I smelled something familiar, something rank and fetid. Dead. Moldering. As the door swept open with a gentle shove from my foot, I hesitated then shifted my gun to my left hand and gripped the flashlight securely in my right. When I had switched it on I stepped carefully into the room, moving my light in wide arcs from right to left, illuminating the whole of the small room with its glow.

In a corner of what now appeared to be a largely empty storage closet, my light captured a truly ghastly sight. Next to a heap of rumpled clothing, a wolf, the size of a large mastiff, lay with milky, vacant eyes staring unblinkingly at the stabbing light. I could hear its shallow breathing in the stillness of the tiny room and watched fascinated as steam rose off its white furry body like vapors on a cooling lake. Its muzzle was curled back in a sort of paralysis showing long dagger-like teeth in the glint of the halogen light. Not daring any movement I froze in place and tried to study this beast as I knew it had to be part of the Skin Walker's pack. I immediately took my shotgun in a firm grip, placing the flashlight under the barrel so I could both see and shoot if necessary.

I felt exposed in the probing glow of the light as I inched my way forward. I stopped short of reaching him when the wolf's eyes rolled slowly in my direction. There was something alarmingly familiar in his eyes. I was nearly undone when I clearly heard it whimper as it gazed up at me. I backed away a bit so I could see the heap of clothing on the floor next to the fallen creature. That's when I saw the same boots that Gus Flores was wearing when we stopped by his bakery earlier. I quickly scanned the rest of the rumpled heap and identified the woolen pants I'd seen under Gus's apron just a few hours ago. Though I didn't want to take the truth in, I had no choice. This was Gus Flores the Ugly Baker!

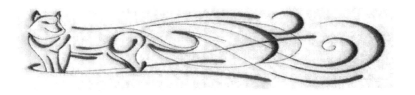

Chapter 25

I felt tears well up in my eyes. I had enjoyed many peaceful visits with Gus in his warm and cozy shop and now, this injured and maybe dying wolf at my feet would be the last memory I'd have of the tiny baker. I knelt down beside the quivering, smoky white body. "Gus," I said softly. We know about the Shaman. We know what he's been doing to people. Please, let us help you stop him, Gus. You're badly hurt and we need to get you out of here."

The baker shifted his corrupted body and whimpered again at the effort. That's when I noticed that his forelegs were resting in a deep pile of the same ash we'd seen in the other bedroom. No! Not resting...his feet, his legs, were gone! He was disintegrating before my eyes. Without thinking I screamed out Jason's name.

As I watched, mesmerized by the slow dissolving into ash of the wretched creature before me, I became aware that my call to Jason had gone unanswered. I expected him to come pounding into the room. When he failed to appear, a feeling of dread came over me and I knew I might very well be on my own now. If Jason was taken by surprise and over-powered, what chance did I have? Was my Magic as strong as the Skin Walker's evil powers?

There was nothing I could do for Gus now and I sensed he wanted me to leave him as what was left of his body was beginning to morph back into his human form. As I watched I realized his body no longer pulsed with the life of that energetic man; a man who had made me feel like a friend. I backed away from what remained of his wolf form and was aware that his eyes had closed before I left him to the dark.

I knew I had already given my location away by calling out for Jason, but I proceeded with as much stealth as possible in any case repeating the *whisper chant* over and over as I moved down the hallway. If nothing else, the mantra seemed to steady my nerves. I had to locate Jason before something awful happened to him; something I couldn't dwell on. With my hands firmly griping my gun and flashlight, I darted back toward the room Jason went to investigate. I passed the open door of the glowing star room and glanced quickly inside. Nothing had changed so I quickly moved to the last room.

I doused my light before entering so I wouldn't present myself as such a clear target. This room was much larger, with several items of furniture and a cold fireplace. I let my eyes adjust to the dimness and the window allowed the pale light reflected from the snow to help me see. I held my gun barrel down, but still in a tight grip so I could easily swing it up at a second's need. That's when I realized how frigid it was in the room and refocused on the window. It was open and the snow was blowing into the room and onto the large bed directly beneath it. Without moving, I pointed the light and gun at the bed, half expecting to see Jason lying there. Instead, I saw that someone, or something, had used it to vault onto the window sill as the pillows were flattened and the bedding was tossed about.

From my memory of the house, the porch roof was likely directly under this room. A perfect landing on the roof and a small leap onto the cushioning snow could mean a clean getaway. I was hoping it was Jason's escape route, and that if I followed I could find him.

But why hadn't Jason called out to me? The howling wind made me feel terribly alone as I left the room and made my way down the unlit staircase. When I reached the bottom step I heard the muffled sound of a door closing. I had been chanting all the way down the stairs so I knew I had masked any sounds I might make in my descent. The front door was still shut so it had to have been the kitchen door that was closed. I worked my chant of stealth and brought my gun up to my shoulder.

Whatever or whoever closed that door was still inside with me. I could feel body heat on my face and hands; some living being was waiting for me around the corner. I stopped the *whisper chant* as stealth was no longer important. I crouched down beside the torn couch and reached my hand onto the floor. The wood was cold and gritty to the touch, but I was able to penetrate this and reach into the ground beneath the house.

I felt the pulsing life of the *Green Mother* begin to course through my hand and up my arm, a heat so intense I gasped as my nerves were seared with white-hot power. The earth's energy imprinted itself on my being, and my eyes became more perceptive even in this semi-darkness. I knew they had changed color into a deep shade of green. In fact, all my senses became more acute.

I was an instrument of the *Green Mother* and walked in her grace and power. I was ready to stare into the very face of death and would prevail over the evil that was waiting like the Reaper, to snuff out my life and Magic. But even knowing I wore the mantel of strength from the *Mother,* I still felt the familiar chill of doubt. Facing demons isn't for the faint of heart, even with Magic. My mother's advice in times like these had always been to "Bring to heal the weakening shadow of doubt and find assuredness by recalling your Sacred Pledge."

Remembering her words now, as if she stood by my side, I recalled my promise to "...*serve in this realm as a Protector pledged in service to the Green Mother.*" I recited each word of my promise with each step I took into the darkness that held another sort of promise...a promise of death.

Chapter 26

As I suspected, the kitchen door was shut. The gory puddle was still inky black on the linoleum, except now it was smeared. There was a set of bloody footprints leading away from it toward the small bathroom. I crept across the room and leveled my gun on the front of the door. "Come out of there!" I yelled trying to sound like a Master Sergeant. There was no movement so I tried another tactic. "Come out and I'll help you if I can. I know about the Shaman and can protect you if you cooperate now."

The door handle slowly turned and with a creak of its hinges, swung open. *This might not have been a good idea* I thought. Standing with his back to me and facing the mirror was Phil, my part-time engineer. He looked back at me from his reflection and said with a sneer, "Hi, boss."

It took me a minute to realize who I saw in the cracked and yellow-veined mirror, but when I recovered my voice I said quietly, "Phil, please turn around slowly and face me." I could see a smile playing at the corners of his mouth like he was fighting the urge to burst out laughing. He turned and leaned against the sink and began to chuckle. I thought I'd heard some pretty scary things screaming and crying out in my time in the woods, but Phil's laugh was so demonic I flinched like he'd struck me in the face.

He saw me jump back and stood straighter. He moved forward a step and I saw the flash of his blood red eyes. His jaw began to drop and elongate and a thick drool began to drip from his open mouth. "Stop right there!" I said in what I hoped was a commanding voice.

He froze and said, "I can wait, but you can't boss."

I had my shotgun aimed at his middle, the largest target always being the best if you don't want to miss. "Phil, I can still help you if you listen to me." He smirked and I noticed his teeth had started to show more prominently and were decidedly more pointed. My sense of smell suddenly went into hyper drive as the stench coming off his body caused me to gag.

"Well boss, it's just you and me, and I don't intend to keep it that way too much longer. You see, I'm hungry. Very hungry. My master won't let us eat without his permission, but he doesn't know about you, just the Sheriff. And he's not long for this world I suspect."

This wasn't good news, but at least I believed Jason was still alive. Phil began to hunch his shoulders and I heard a distinctive cracking and shifting as his bones twisted and warped into new configurations. I shook myself mentally as I was becoming mesmerized by his transformation from mousy man into ferocious werewolf.

I knew my magic incantations would need the strength of the *Green Mother* to instill her full power into my words. Without taking my eyes or gun off this terrible changeling, I backed up to the kitchen door and using my free hand turned the knob. I knew the trees were close to the house and barely got my hand on the mossy trunk of the one nearest when Phil was gone and I was facing the werewolf he'd become.

My ward was immediate and powerful. *"Coill crann,"* I screamed like my life depended on it, and by all the gods it did! My hand shifted from flesh to bark as it was absorbed into the wood of the tree and the *Mother's* gifts rushed into me like a fast flowing river. The shotgun fell from my right hand along with the lighted flashlight which rolled away to be smothered by a deep drift. I became an electric transmitter, with a high voltage current running along my nerve endings. Anything that touched me would be instantly charred.

The werewolf was salivating heavily. His mouth was drawn back into a toothy snarl. In a blur of motion he sprang for my throat and the moment he touched my outstretched hand, burst into a green all-consuming flame that burned with the intensity of a small sun, until there was only a pile of Phil-ash at my feet.

Now, there could be no doubt that the Shaman had his wicked coils wrapped around the very heart of my new home town, right into and including my new radio station and staff. And I understood that the Dark Magic being practiced here would have to be destroyed utterly, or every person living in Iron Mountain was at risk of howling at the moon!

I pulled my fuzzy knit hat down firmly over my ears and hunched my shoulders as deeply as I could into my heavy woolen coat. I had to get to the front of the house to pick up the trail that I hoped would lead me to Jason. I retrieved my flashlight from under the snow mound, not wanting to deplete my energy further by using green fire to light the way. Rather than stumble around in the back of the house I detoured through the kitchen and out the front door.

I stepped off the wooden porch, sagging more perilously with the weight of the snow drifting over it. There were prints just barely visible a few feet off to the left and I hurried over to examine them before they could be obscured by the storm that had become unnaturally powerful. I knew its savage nature was not of the *Mother* as I had touched her discontent when she filled me with her awesome fire.

I saw what looked like huge paw prints next to what was clearly a heavy boot print. Both were filling in quickly, but I made out several more moving off in the direction of the Iron Mountain Coal Mine. Jason had pointed out the mine's location earlier as we drove up here and from my reckoning of the area, it was less-than a quarter mile in the direction of the prints.

While beginning to follow the prints, my mind took one of its fights of fancy and I started to think about my dad. My father had an uncanny sense of direction and moved through the wild forests like a wood nymph out for a stroll. My mother joked, he could find his way to any deer blind in the woods, during a hurricane, with his eyes blindfolded, but he couldn't find the front door of his house when the roof needed repairing. He always replied to these challenges with, "That's why we have Magic!" Of course with nosey neighbors that might happen along, that wasn't always an option.

He often told me that I'd inherited his "unique questing skills" when he was training me in "*riastrad*", the Magic art of using nature to camouflage our presence. I loved the excitement of following sign and now I would use my instincts to follow the trail of two beings, one human, one dangerous werewolf.

My focus was entirely on the environment and I knew my quarry was close. While searching the ground ahead of me I kept a keen eye and alert ear to any sound that might give away a location. I felt sure I was following Jason because of the deep boot impressions, but the large paw prints that seemed to be placed within inches of his were confounding my sense of reason. Why would one of the Shaman's wolf pack be walking with Jason through the woods to the coal mine? Unless…

Then I spotted movement ahead through a cluster of evergreens, snow-burdened branches sweeping the ground with every gust of wind. With one of the stronger burst of wind, the trees bowed lower and I clearly made out the back of Jason's bare head and his brown Sheriff's coat. Something made me wait before I called out to him and that's when Big Red came into view. He padded up to Jason's side and his head reached Jason's shoulder. Having seen him from a distance, I had no idea Big Red was so huge! *Wow!* I thought to myself. *Jason seems to have an ally.* I wasn't surprised as we had figured out that the real identity of Big Red was Jason's faithful Deputy. Leo had already destroyed one wolfman and now it appeared he was part of the hunt for his old Master, the Skin Walker.

I watched from behind a large spruce to be certain that this was a safe alliance to join. Jason seemed fine, with nothing to indicate he'd been in a battle for his life. As I followed, far enough away to be undetected, I heard a deep, other-worldly sound riding the dark winds. The moon had moved off to hover over what looked like a gash in the face of the stone, the entrance to the Iron Mountain Coal Mine.

The sound had come from Big Red as he arched his neck back and howled like the wolf he was. The sound was answered moments later by another howl, and, as Jason stood transfixed, the chorus was joined by at least two other voices. *This must be the rest of the Skin Walker's wolf pack* I thought.

My heart was doing a tattoo on my ribs as the answering howls echoed within the storm raging around me. Jason seemed unafraid of the wolf calls, only standing quietly at Big Red's side. It was as if he was some kind of lord of the forest, waiting for his vassals to do his bidding.

Wait. *NO!* I screamed in my head. *Not Jason!*

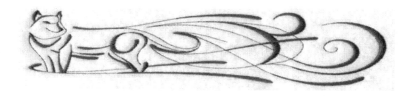

Chapter 27

As I crouched behind the veil of heavily blanketed evergreens, I began to formulate a plan to destroy the Skin Walker and rescue Jason, if he needed rescuing. For both our sakes, I prayed to the *Mother* that he did. The alternative was unthinkable.

I hadn't mentioned to Jason that my dad had experiences with Skin Walkers during his youth, but in Ireland they were known to shift into docile animals that dulled the caution of a potential victim. These shifters known as *athelmorts*, were fabled creatures in old Europe and that's probably how they made their entrance onto the American scene. My father said according to Indian myth, one method of destroying a Skin Walker was by saying his full name out loud, sort of like placing a mirror in front of them so they had to acknowledge their humanity. I remembered reading the account of the old Indian who had come to Iron Mountain around 1840. His strange name struck me as a portent of his evil nature and now I unconsciously whispered it into the night: "Joseph Moon Slayer".

Right then, however, I had to refocus on Jason's situation. He actually seemed in less danger than I did at the moment. I was keenly aware that my only friend may have joined forces with the evil ones, to find his long lost brother. If that was the case, my own safety was in real jeopardy.

Jason and Big Red began to move forward. The giant wolf lopped easily over the snow with his splayed, furry paws. Jason was less graceful in the drifts as he struggled to free his legs and feet from the deep, white quagmire. As they progressed toward the mouth of the coal mine, I scurried from drift to tree, to keep up with them. Suddenly, just as I was ducking behind a large rock on the approach to the Shaman's lair, Big Red stopped short and slowly turned his head around. His nose was pointed in my direction and I was beginning to regret my spurt of perfume and deodorant.

Without hesitation, I whispered into the wind *"cuaifeach neart"* in the ancient tongue of the Gaelic Druid Mage. It was constructed in a quick burst of syllables, each word calling down the force of nature to conceal my presence from any peering eye. The wind, already screaming in my ears, picked up to near gale force strength and with it, the snow, swirling like a crystal whirling dervish. With the wind howling louder, the two figures began to move off toward the mouth of the mine and I was able to use their movement to conceal my own as I followed at a discreet distance. I still chanted so as to hide in the whirlwind of flakes until they entered the mine.

There wasn't much point in counting on Jason's help if I got caught in a serious situation, but I still had that strange feeling of security as far as Big Red was concerned. He might not be the one to attack me if I was discovered, but he was still counted among the Skin Walker's pack and an unknown entity if his loyalty was challenged.

I was now directly outside the mouth of the mine and carefully stepped into the passageway. I looked back briefly over my shoulder at the footprints I had left and was relieved to see they were being obliterated by the furor of snow and wind. Now I crouched lower as I moved forward into the darkness of the cave's opening. There was no sign of either Big Red or Jason so I stopped and stood still in the dim entryway to listen for movement ahead. *There!* The unmistakable clanking as a shaft elevator door closed and then the whir of the machine's motor as it began its descent.

Considering how long ago this mine closed down, it sure has sturdy equipment! I thought with a frown. I suspected that a recently made pack member was maintaining things so that victims could be hidden away quickly.

I'd have to find another way down to track them, unless I risked bringing the elevator back up. I started following the rail line used to move the coal out of the depths of the mine, hoping to find another shaft elevator toward the back of the main tunnel. The coal cars were not all empty. Some were half full of chunks of black rocks torn from the heart of the mine. As I kept my flashlight pointed downward I happened to cast a brief glow over one of the carts. That's when I saw a boot clad foot dangling over the side.

I stepped close enough to illuminate the interior of the cart and saw what looked like a mangled heap of clothing clinging to the skeleton of what must have been a large man. I'm not the squeamish type, but there was something unsettling about finding a body dressed in rotting clothing that was so old fashioned it was clearly from another century. My immediate thought was that he was an old mountain man. There was a ratty fur cap, cocked over his skull in a bizarrely jaunty fashion, a heavy leather boot that hung loosely from his one projecting skeletal foot and what was left of a much chewed on plaid woolen coat was all that covered his remains.

It looked like he'd been dumped along with his rifle, which poked out of the coal dusted cart behind his body. I felt a chill as I stood contemplating this rather bizarre tableau. It was as if this man was left as a warning to anyone who would dare enter the cloying darkness of the Iron Mountain Coal Mine. All that was lacking was a sign reading, "This could be YOU!"

After studying the skelctal remains of "the mountain man," I moved silently past the remaining coal carts and back into the deeper recesses of the tunnel. I kept my light on, but occasionally pointed it upward toward the ceiling of the tunnel to insure the height wouldn't drop off precipitously leaving me with a lump on my head and a possible disorientation I couldn't afford to suffer under the circumstances. I needed a clear head and strong will. The gun helped supply most of my courage. Along with the *whisper chant* that I was practically humming, hoping to mask my presence and movements.

As I moved forward, I became aware of a change in level. The pitch of the floor seemed to fall sharply and I found myself moving closer to the damp walls to help steady my footing. I was definitely on my way down to the lower levels of the mine.

Using the flashlight continuously was going to be risky so I scouted ahead with quick shafts of light and then switched it off, feeling my way along the rocky surface, trying to remember the contours of the tunnel ahead. I was afraid to alert the Shaman to my presence by using any kind of Magic in case he was like other Magic users and sensitive to a force at work in the vacinity. After several painfully slow minutes of this, I turned the light back on, shielding the beam with my hand while shifting the gun in my grip so as not to drop it. Suddenly, the amber light from my flashlight bounced back at me from what appeared to be a dead end.

I need to back-track out of this I thought as I started to turn, but a sharp glint of metal on the wall's rough surface, stopped me in my tracks. It was some sort of handle jutting out only a hair's breath and would have been overlooked by me except for the light catching its brassy sheen. This had to be some kind of hidden passage into the depths of the mine and when I opened the secret door I would likely have to face the powerful Shaman and his pack of werewolves alone.

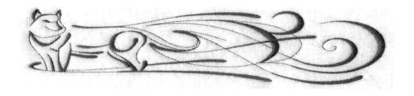

Chapter 28

I heard nothing but my own quickened breath, so I leaned my riffle against the wall and shinning the flashlight on the small handle, I began to pull and twist until I heard a click. What had appeared to be a solid wall slid silently forward and to the right. I knew I had to move quickly, but was afraid the secret door would slam, leaving me locked in the Skin Walker's lair with only my gun and a flickering flashlight. *Oh, no!* I thought frantically. I hadn't noticed that the light was beginning to dim as the battery started to lose its charge. This was the time to make a little Magic happen and I had to act fast and just chance that it would go undetected if the Shaman was preoccupied with his newest victim.

A greenish light spilling weakly from the hidden entryway helped me see while I frantically tore at the buttons of my coat and wrapped it around my failing flashlight. Then, lodging it at the entrance I whispered softly, *"Bilebiss,"* as my coat and flashlight fused into a solid log of wood. It felt good to use my Magic, but I didn't want to chance it further so decided to rely on the anemic green illuminating the passage.

Grabbing my gun I threw myself into the opening as the door began to go back down and held my breath as it reached my make-shift obstruction. It stopped as if by some unseen sensor and reversed itself. I hoped it would hold until I grabbed my coat and that would only happen if I was running for my life!

The unnatural light seemed to be coming from the walls of a large cavern. I stopped to orient myself to my new surroundings and to make sure my gun was ready to fire. In the deep silence of the mine I heard what sounded like Jason's voice coming from a branch off the passage I was following. I kept close to the wall and crept forward for another three minutes until I crouched just outside what could only be described as a small cell. Jason was stretched out on a long table, his legs and arms tied with a heavy rope. He was talking urgently to his guard.

"Leo, for the love of all things sacred to you, cut these ropes before it's too late for me to help you."

Just then, a large shadow passed over the Sheriff. I pulled back and tried to push myself into the rock as far as possible while I watched and barely exhaled. Moving above Jason's vulnerable body was what had to be the Skin Walker, diving at him in his current form of an impossibly large and hideous cave bat. He swooped in from the height of the cave's ceiling where he had likely been hanging while he observed his latest captive. He pulled up just at the last moment, causing Jason to jerk in a spasm of startled fear.

He landed with a thud on the dirt floor next to the prisoner and with his wings pulled over his bowed head, began to transform back into his human form--if that's what you could call what I saw after his transition from giant bat to man.

I was afraid to blink as I watched the large bat, repulsive enough, turn into a stooped and wizened relic of a man. His skin hung like a pale red cloak from his arms and his head resembled a shrunken red apple left to dry in the last days of autumn sun. Before I could look at his lower body, he had snatched up a rough looking blanket from the floor beside Jason. I was rather relieved that he spared me any further anatomy study. I noted that when he grabbed the blanket, he moved in a blur, springing like a coiled snake. I had to adjust my thinking of him from an ancient man to a witch with dark powers if I was going to get Jason and myself out of here alive. Underestimating the Skin Walker would be a serious and deadly mistake.

In his human form as Indian Shaman, the Skin Walker approached the table and the restrained prisoner. He spoke in a hissing whisper. "So. We meet. It was unwise for you to hunt me down, Sheriff. You lawmen are a stupid breed."

Jason stiffened and replied "We uphold the laws of the people while you destroy all that is good."

The Shaman made a sickly gurgling sound that was probably his attempt to laugh.

"I have used your own Deputy these many years past to do my bidding, Sheriff, and he still serves only my will. You are nothing to me but an annoyance, like a small biting insect. And like an insect, I can crush the life out of you." With that, the old man raised his hand and held it over Jason's chest. I could hear Jason's breathing becoming more labored and after less than a minute, he began to gasp for air.

Just as I was about to leap out of hiding, Big Red stepped into view and growled deep in his throat. Distracted from his torture spell the Shaman screeched like a wounded cat.

"You fool," shouted the ancient Indian in a raspy voice. "Get away from me and guard the entrance to the mine. My work here is just beginning. This white man will welcome his death when I finally permit it to take him. Now, get out of here before I hang your pelt next to the others!"

Others? I thought frantically. This meant he'd already destroyed some of his pack. Why? And why had Big Red switched his allegiance back to his evil Master? Those questions would have to wait to be answered. Now I had to find a way to save Jason from unspeakable torture and certain death.

I knew if Big Red saw me he'd be forced to help me, or I'd be forced to kill him. I had to act fast. Since the Shaman had not detected my earlier use of magic, I backed away from the cell, camouflaging my movements with a *whisper chant.* I was relieved to find a large enough fissure in the tunnel wall to slide in sideways.

A minute later the outsized red wolf sauntered past, but I had the distinct feeling he sensed my presence as his massive head turned ever so slightly in my direction. I held my breath and slowed my heartbeat, afraid he'd hear the thumping, until he was well past. Even if I killed the Skin Walker, we'd have to deal with Big Red before we were home free, unless I was right about his loyalty to Jason. The red glint of his eyes was anything but reassuring!

I arrived back at my original hiding place in time to hear Jason say, "What did you do with the people you've been kidnapping over all these years? You must be what? 113 by now, old man? You've stolen the lives of dozens of innocent folks over that time." I wondered why Jason was taunting him.

The Shaman did his version of a chuckle again. "I have many needs as a powerful Shaman and these people were mine to take and to rule. Many had been turned like your own trusted Deputy was to serve as part of my pack. And my age is as ancient as my power." I decided the Shaman was actually enjoying the opportunity to brag about himself and that's why he wasn't inflicting more punishment on Jason. I also knew that wouldn't last long.

Jason asked about the ash we found in Prescott's house. It was like he was trying to keep the Shaman talking to gain some time. Maybe Jason believed I'd be able to help him, but that seemed unlikely. He wouldn't know about my discovery of the secret doorway to this part of the mine.

"Were those the ashes of some of the people you've been holding here?" The Shaman had his back to the opening of the cell, but I knew Jason would be able to see me if I stepped out a bit. I needed him to keep the Shaman distracted so I could take him by surprise.

"You have a keen eye, Sheriff." He gave a quick snort of amusement. "Though it will do you no good now. My pack was becoming weak and changing without my permission. Even the white snake, Prescott, began to secretly study the heavens to bring more power to himself, outside of my pack and control. The white dog was searching the stars so that he could overpower me in my weakest form as a human. Weak, just as you are weak, sheriff."

Jason seemed to be doing something with the rope tied around his hands as the Shaman ranted on about Prescott and circled the table and his prisoner. He was describing how Prescott would live long enough to feel his skin being peeled away from his puny body when I saw the knotted rope fall open. Jason quickly grabbed the end to conceal the fact his hands were free. I knew I had to act now to give him time to finish freeing himself.

"Prescott could never be as evil as you, old man. According to your own legends, you had to kill someone close to you to become a true Skin Walker. Who was it?"

The Shaman stopped his pacing and stared down at Jason. "You know much for a feeble white man, but what does it matter now? You will die shortly and I've always found pride in my story. My father needed only one strong son to succeed him as chief, so I took my weak older brother out hunting and only I came back to our father's lodge. Because of my many coups in battle, I easily proved my strength to my father and the clan."

He seemed smug until Jason said "And then, did you have to run like a rabbit when they found out about the dark magic you called upon for strength?"

I thought the Shaman would punish Jason's insult, but he merely sneered and drew the ratty blanket closer around his putrid body.

That was it. The smell from the basement at the radio station. He smelled like those beasts!"

"I had the power to destroy all of them, but I left to create my own pack and live as I should, the only great Shaman of my tribe. They are all dust now, dirt under my feet and I have walked in power these many moons."

Jason chuckled then quietly said, "You are barely alive and have given your spirit to rule a pack of captive wolf-men while you hide like a prairie dog deep in his burrow."

It was time to act. The ancient Indian was beginning to sound even crazier as he raved on about how he could control all of life and all humans would obey him. I decided not to show myself immediately so I slunk back to the crevice in the wall and using the natural echo chamber provided by the tunnel I called out his name using my voice control to deepen the pitch. "*Joseph Moon Slayer, hear your name!*" His name echoed and bounced off the greenish cell walls. I said his name again. "*Joseph Moon Slayer, you shall die!*"

I heard the Shaman scream out as if his life was being sucked out of his withered body. I knew he was now vulnerable to my bullets and it was time to use my other weapon. I came into the cell and saw the Shaman in a spasm on the cave floor. He was foaming at the mouth like a rabid animal and I knew I had to take a head shot to truly destroy him. I pointed and took a deep, slowing breath and then pulled the trigger.

The blast from the shotgun deafened me momentarily and I realized it would likely alert any of the pack that might be in the mine. I quickly muffled any sound reverberation from the shot, holding out my free hand and binding the sound to the tunnel walls; then turned my attention to the table where Jason lay looking stunned and confused.

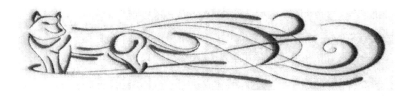

Chapter 29

Jason was so surprised to see me and to witness what I had just done that he lay immobile for a minute. Then, he threw back the rope that had been on his legs, but not truly tied. He explained as he threw them aside and got down from the table that Leo had helped him by pretending to remain in the Skin Walker's power. He had taken Jason to the cell as if he was his prisoner and put the ropes around his feet and hands to make it look realistic. According to Leo, who kept his human form long enough to carry out the charade, the old Indian had left to finish destroying his dwindling pack. They had all started to act more human and less wolf-like and were changing into human form more often despite the Shaman's commands and threats. Leo himself had destroyed as many of the pack as he could because they were still violent and infected with the evil of the Skin Walker's magic. And it gave him credibility with the crazed Shaman as to his own loyalty.

Jason walked over to where the Shaman had fallen after hearing me call out his mortal name. He seemed to be memorizing what lay on the dirt floor. There was nothing left of the Skin Walker, but a pile of ash showing from under the ratty blanket. I stood across from the opening to the cell and Jason came over and gently removed the rifle from my stiffening fingers. He leaned it against the tunnel wall and gave me a big bear hug. I seemed to be waking from a dream and suddenly realized what I had just done. I was shaking from head to foot like a wet dog that was caught in the rain. I felt a warm, tingling sensation circling my shoulders as Jason held me close.

"It's ok, Cathleen," Jason said softly. I'm alright now; we're alright now."

I looked up at him and said, "Jason, we still have Leo to deal with if he's still a werewolf. We have to destroy every one of them." I sounded almost hysterical even to myself, so I bit off my next comment before I uttered an insensitive comment about his brother. Jason took hold of my elbow and my gun and steered me away from the cell and away from the grisly remains.

The greenish light was enough for me to get us back to the secret door without using my own *green fire*. I was relieved to see that my make-shift obstruction was still in place and the door hadn't slid closed. I whispered the words to unbind my coat and flashlight and return them to their former state just as we passed through the door. It immediately retracted into the cave floor with a loud thud, reminding me how close we had come to being trapped if my rigged door stop had failed.

I was happy to have my heavy coat back on and buttoned it up close to my chin as we walked as quickly as we could through the murky tunnels. Jason's own flashlight was long gone and mine was sputtering like a candle in a breeze. Neither of us spoke until we saw a dim light that told us we were nearing the mine's entrance. We were now standing next to the coal cars and I knew it was only a short walk before we had the answer to my questions about Leo. *If we find Leo in his werewolf form what will Jason do,* I wondered as we moved carefully toward the front of the mine.

As we passed the car that held the remains of the mountain man, Jason stopped and turned the failing light on the remains. In a hushed voice he said, "This guy was the old Sheriff of Iron Mountain back in 1890 something. He went missing along with his two deputies. They came up here loaded for bear, but after two weeks the people gave up on them ever returning, just like the others that went missing."

It seemed peculiar to me that Jason would stop to give me a quick history lesson, but I told him I thought he looked like a relic from the past. Jason spoke again after studying the skeletal remains a moment longer. "I was hoping we'd find some trace of my brother, but I think he was destroyed by the Skin Walker along with the rest of the people he turned."

I felt very sure Jason was right, but I knew how he must be hurting so said nothing. As we made our way past the coal cars we heard someone shout out Jason's name. It was Leo who by now had transformed back to his human form. Jason turned to me and said softly, "Stay here until I call for you Cathleen. I want to be sure it's safe before we let Leo know you are here with me."

I wanted to give him my rifle, but he said Leo would guess I was with him and he handed it back to me saying, "Just stay put until you hear me call your name." With that, he turned and quickly disappeared into the shadows of the last coal cars.

Waiting alone in the murky light, my mind started to wander as I listened to Jason's boots scrape up the rock strewn incline toward to the mouth of the mine. Suddenly, I felt like I had been slapped awake. *Wait a minute. How could he know that was a Sheriff from the 1800s? I never saw a badge! And he seemed very comfortable telling me to keep the gun, but he told me Leo already knew I was here!*

My senses were screaming that something was very wrong with this situation. I wanted to cling to my feeling of safety knowing Jason was alright and with me. But why was he so determined I stay behind and not show myself? I tightened my grip on the gun. I shivered as I recalled that the Skin Walker could take on many forms, but so too could his pack. Did I just escape the Shaman with one of his henchmen? And if so, who was he *really,* and where was Jason Tate?

I crept forward and strained to hear what was going on outside the mine. When I could see the blowing snow reflected in the hovering moon's pale light, I made my way until I was behind the first coal car. It rested at an angle that gave me a clear view without exposing my position.

The wind had died down some and I was able to see two men standing over what looked like a third man. He was lying on the ground and from the look of the snow covering his coat and legs he'd been there for a while. "You can drop your disguise now, Jeff. Jason can't hurt you anymore." It was Leo speaking to the man I'd just rescued. The man who looked like Jason now laughed and kicked out at the prone figure.

"Jason never could hurt me." He laughed and kicked the still body on the ground again, this time harder and I heard a gasp of pain and a long groan. I still couldn't see who the injured man was, but had no doubt it was the handsome Sheriff.

"Your brother only wanted to save you from the Skin Walker, Jeff. That's all he ever wanted."

"Shut up, Leo!" Jeff shouted. He left me up here all these years! But I survived and the Shaman made me his Alpha! I am powerful and strong. Not like the weakling I was when I wandered up here. By the way, thanks for telling me about the ashes at Prescott's house. That's when I figured out that the Shaman had been killing off our pack members. Less for me to worry about hunting down."

Leo said, "Jeff, you and I both know there is no way out of here alive." Jeff laughed and it sounded strange and wrong, coming out of what looked like Jason's mouth. "I am stronger now than when I got turned, Leo. You remember that don't you Leo? You're the wolf that turned me!"

Leo started to reply," That wasn't…" but stopped when Jeff hunched over, his arms reaching to the ground and his head thrown back. Suddenly, without warning Jeff turned and stared in my direction. He took two steps toward my hiding place and I knew he'd smelled me. He'd begun to change into his werewolf form and I was almost relieved he didn't look like the man I'd come to care about so much.

I began a breathless spell, using the power of the elements deep within the ground, of strength and darkness, to blur my presence and become absorbed into my surroundings. I reached out to the Mother to hear my words of need.

The smell of old coal dust filled my nose and I felt my body become rigid as it was camouflaged behind the coal car; taking on the appearance of the mine walls. I had heard my father do this enchantment hundreds of times as he concealed us while we hunted game more dangerous than deer. I wasn't sure I knew the old tongue well enough to cast this spell, but my life and the real Jason's life, depended on it. *"Bridget, Dagda, shield me from eye, smell, sound."* I whispered the words as they flowed according to my bidding from my subconscious mind to my tongue.

By the time I was through with the incantation, Jeff had reverted back into his werewolf form completely and was covered in thick, black fur. His snout was pulled away from long, yellow teeth. He stopped at the entrance and peered into the dank, semi-dark of the mine entrance. He started to come forward and seemed headed right for me as I stood plastered against the wall. I heard him snarl and saw him begin to salivate, his mouth dripping with an evil hunger.

As I watched, transfixed to the wall by my spell, I saw a red streak of movement. Leo! He had taken his own wolf form and was now charging headlong into Jeff. Just as he was about to lunge, the black werewolf turned and with a sweep of his fore leg, knocked Big Red into a snow drift 10 feet away.

Oh, no! I thought. Big Red sprang back to his feet so quickly I barely registered the movement. He immediately began to circle the black werewolf, snarling a low guttural growl all the while. The black wolf was smaller than Big Red, but looked like he outweighed him by a good 15 pounds. They took each other's measure while I stared in my frozen state; unable to move and barely breathing for fear of discovery.

Just as Big Red looked ready to charge, the brittle air was filled with a desperate cry. "NO!" It was Jason, struggling to regain his feet. He called again. "No, Leo! Please. Not Jeff." At that distraction, the black wolf covered the space that separated them and in a blink had his teeth into Big Red's throat. With an awful scream of pain, the red werewolf fell to the ground with the black wolf pressing down on his prone body. The blood was everywhere as the black werewolf tore into Big Red like the killing machine he was. It was over in less than a minute and I knew Big Red was no more. He was still twitching as his life seeped dark red into the frozen ground.

In that instant Jason seemed to come fully alert to the death and watched in horror as Big Red began to turn back to his human form as his friend and Deputy, Leo, and then gradually began to dissolve into grey ash. The wind blew his remains away with a final gust, until only its relentless howl occupied the space where Leo had died.

As if he was of no more significance than the slain deputy, the black werewolf turned his back to Jason who seemed unable to move. He appeared to be completely immobilized by the savage attack he had just witnessed.

I knew that I had only seconds. He was moving back toward me. With this realization, I broke free of the spell and standing detached from the tunnel wall, pointed my rifle in the direction of the fast approaching werewolf. I took a second to inhale, and as I exhaled, pulled the trigger.

The blast was deafening as it bounced off the dark walls of the mine. The charging werewolf vanished behind a curtain of red and seemed to vaporize, like so much mist. When the smoke from my gun cleared I saw Jason, dragging his left leg, trying to make his way over to what had been his brother. He stood with a painful effort over the form as it faded into its human body and then into dead

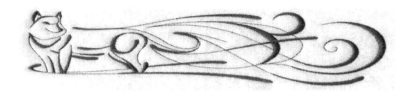

Chapter 30

Jason and I headed back to his SUV like two soldiers returning from the front. He dragged his left leg as it had a deep gash just below his kneecap. He leaned heavily on my shoulder and we stopped often to rest on fallen logs or flat rocks. We didn't speak. There was nothing either of us wanted to say out loud. We were still in shock, disbelief, horror, too many conflicted emotions to process all at once.

It was getting light by the time we sighted Prescott's house and Jason's snow-covered squad car parked in front. The snow had let up and was only dusting us with the occasional flurry by the time we opened the doors to his vehicle. Jason now turned to me and said simply, "You drive," as he handed me his keys.

The trip back down the mountain was less perilous with the dawn. Fading stars gave way to a sunrise of pale rose and deepest pinks, making the scene one of unblemished peace and beauty. I had a firm grip on the wheel as the roads had no boundaries save the tree line. Jason sat hunched into his coat though it was still heavy with wet snow. His hair was wet and sticking to his neck as the result of the warming vehicle. I had the heater on full blast. We both continued to defrost until our seats turned damp with the melt-off.

I gave him a sidelong glance before turning back to the steep drive ahead. "Jason, are you in much pain from your leg?"

"I'll be ok, Cathleen. I was sitting here trying to figure out what just happened back there, but it's really clear enough." He moved his leg with his hands to adjust for better comfort. "I think I always knew that Jeff had been taken by the Skin Walker, but I never wanted to believe he could be turned. I hoped he was dead rather than that."

I listened without any comment so he would go on talking. I knew that saying his feelings out loud was the beginning of his healing.

"I used to go up there around the mine every weekend I could for two years, searching for Jeff. I used the mine like my pivot and plotted my range of searching accordingly. I covered miles of mountain country during that time. I never saw any sign of him, just lots of tracks and kill sites. The Shaman was very skilled at planting false leads for any would-be tracker. I searched mostly west of the mine itself as that's where all the clues led. I never went deep into the mine, never as far in as the coal cars, as it was sealed up back then and as a 16 year old kid, I was alone and pretty scared.

When I found Leo at Prescott's place, he told me he had shaken free of the Shaman's power long ago and had been acting like a guardian to the folks in town. He felt it was his sworn duty as my Deputy to protect us. Jason gave a quick, sharp laugh, shaking his head in amazement. "My own Deputy..."

Jason sat quietly for several minutes looking out the window. His face was as bleak as the landscape and I felt awkward asking, but I had to know. "Did Leo ever try to hurt you when you discovered him at Prescott's?"

He gave me a quick look and answered. "Leo was in his human form then and didn't change until we went after the Shaman together. He told me he only wanted to protect us, you especially I think, since he seemed very upset that I let you go back up the mountain. Since we were already there, he agreed to show me the way into the lair below the old mine. I was supposed to pretend that he'd captured me and was bringing me in for his Master to deal with.

He was leaving me in that cell when Jeff showed up. I was so excited that he was still alive I guess I didn't focus on just how that was possible. Jeff was a grown man, but I recognized him immediately. We reunited like long lost brothers as you'd expect while Leo just stood there watching. I didn't realize his suspicion because I was so happy and relieved.

I described our plan to Jeff, believing he was going to help us destroy his Master. My brother told Leo to find the Shaman so we could carry it out quickly. I remember now how hesitant Leo was to leave me. When he finally did, Jeff turned into...that creature, and attacked me. I never saw it coming and was too shocked to believe what was happening."

Jason paused and slicked his hair back from his forehead before going on. "He must have dragged me outside of the mine while I was unconscious. I believe Jeff wanted to take the Shaman's place and wanted us to destroy him so he wouldn't have to expose himself to the Shaman's powers. That's why he helped you, Cathleen. He used your courage as his own weapon."

I had only one more question. "Why didn't Leo just attack the Skin Walker himself, Jason?" "Because," he answered, "the Skin Walker was careful never to be in his vulnerable human form when he was around any of the pack. He was too powerful in his other shapes for Leo to fight and live to tell the tale."

We drove in silence for a while and I tried to keep myself from asking Jason more questions as I knew he was still in deep shock at the death of both his brother and Leo. Without turning to me Jason said, "Cathleen, I know you had no choice back there. He would have killed you and me both." I gripped the wheel tighter as I responded.

"I tried to conceal myself Jason, so I wouldn't have to shoot, but he seemed to sense my hiding place."

He lowered his head, staring at his folded hands, and said, "It really wasn't Jeff up there. I know that Jeff died as soon as he was turned into that evil monster that you killed. He was no better than the Shaman and from what Leo told me when he found me wounded outside the mine, he was almost worse. He wanted to take total control of the pack and was planning to turn more of the folks from town."

It was hard to hear the sadness and resignation in Jason's voice, but I listened as he continued in a subdued voice. "What I haven't figured out yet is why Jeff accused Leo of turning him. Leo wasn't even here when Jeff went missing. He was living two counties over in Trapperville. Actually, I only knew Leo when he moved to Iron Mountain with his family and he started going to our high school in junior year."

"Gee", I said, "you and Leo went back a long time, Jason."

"Yeah," he mumbled, distracted. Then, "There's something wrong here, Cathleen. We need to go back up to the mine."

"Jason, are you crazy?" I demanded as I gave him a look of utter disbelief. The *last* thing I wanted to do was return to that terrible place. But Jason outlined his reasoning so persuasively that I found myself looking for a safe place to turn around.

Jason sensed my fear and reluctance to return to that evil hideout, and reached over to place a reassuring hand on my shoulder. "Cathleen, it'll be alright. We still have plenty of ammo and if there's still something left alive up there that poses a threat, I promise you, we'll take it out!" I was not totally assured, but knew that if there was even one of the Shaman's pack left alive, no one would be safe in Iron Mountain.

Chapter 31

By now the sun was moving overhead and our drive became less perilous as I could easily see the pattern of a roadway. Prescott's house came into view, but Jason told me to keep driving toward the mine as his SUV was definitely a sturdy off-road vehicle and the way there was fairly flat.

As we crept up to the mouth of the mine, Jason said, "Let's not get too close. I don't want the sound of our motor to alert anyone we're here." With that, he carefully stepped out of the vehicle, placing his injured leg softly on the snow-packed ground. It had stopped bleeding and when he gradually put some weight on it, he was unable to hide a quick grimace, but took a deep breath and motioned me to move out.

We still had our rifles with us and I had grabbed extra bullets for each of us from the back seat. Jason seemed to be doing all right as we approached under cover from the boulders and any trees close to the opening. Except for the occasional bird call, it was deathly quiet. I looked around and noticed that all trace of Leo and Jeff had completely disappeared. In fact, there was no remaining evidence of clothing, blood or trampled ground. Someone had cleaned the site to a nearly pristine condition.

I spotted something shinny poking out from under the lip of a large grey boulder. It was probably overlooked in the semi-darkness at the time of the clean sweep someone made of the place. When I reached down to retrieve it, I realized it was a fancy button off a sport coat. I slipped it unnoticed into my pocket as I followed Jason into the mine.

"Jason, where are we going?"

He answered, "The elevator is back up here. That's how Jeff was able to move me and I don't think I can manage to get back down there any other way."

"If someone is down there they'll hear us coming," I said, hoping my fear wasn't too apparent.

"Don't worry," he said, "whoever is down there is licking his wounds about now."

"What do you mean?" I asked, as we loaded into the cage and started our descent.

In the dimming light I could barely make out his features, but his answer was very clear. "Leo and I left a trap down there for any wolf that might have escaped him or the Shaman. We used a pelt from a pack member that met his end by being skinned alive, something the Shaman seemed to enjoy doing on occasion. Leo put his scent on it good and strong and we shoved it across from a camouflaged pit. If someone, or something, tried to grab it, they'd fall into the pit. It might not kill them, but would slow them down."

We both switched on our flashlights with the back-up batteries firmly installed now. The light was comforting and disorienting at the same time. "Jason, I have a better way." With that I brought *green fire* to my left hand after putting the flashlight on the cage floor. "That's a whole lot easier on our eyes." I said, searching his face for any sense of alarm. He seemed pretty comfortable with the idea of me holding a small flame in my hand to light our way.

"Good idea, Cathleen." he said with a small grin." He spoke softly now as we had hit bottom with a jolt. I could hear the bullets jingle in our pockets.

I moved close to him and whispered, "Do you know who's down here?"

"I have my hunches and hope I'm wrong, but if not, it'll take a lot to bring him down."

Our eyes were gradually adjusting to the weak greenish lighting coming from the walls of the tunnels and my *green fire*. We crept forward, our guns ready to shoot as we had already chambered a bullet before entering the mine. I felt ahead with my deepest senses trying to discover even a hint of who, or what, lay in store for us. I couldn't shake the feeling that we were moving through a living, green slime. The walls were coated with thick moisture that had a greasy look and seemed to pulsate in the pale light. I felt our breath clinging to the air and then smelled another life force, and the breath of evil.

No word was spoken, but I felt Jason go very still and his body tensed as we stopped, shoulder to shoulder. He leaned close to my ear and even then was barely audible, "He's ahead of us about 20 feet."

I closed my hand over the green flame immediately and we stood motionless. I had picked up on the presence a minute before Jason's warning and was ready to shoot, but nodded my head automatically. Whoever was ahead of us was moving in a low crouch. "Not human," I whispered in Jason's ear. The creature stopped moving and seemed to be rising into a standing position. He was enormous, filling the opening ahead with a massive body. Jason screamed as he switched his flashlight back on, "He's charging, fire!"

The werewolf covered the twenty feet in the time it took me to blink. His demonic roar bounced off the sides of the mine and slammed into our faces, shattering our ears. We braced our bodies and in our sudden deafness we met him with a wall of bullets.

When we saw him drop, we backed up a foot or two. The body was lying in the twin glow from Jason's flashlight and the *green fire* I suddenly held in my hand. It's larger flame waivered as I tried to calm myself down after the charge by taking deep breaths of the stale, damp air. Jason looked at it briefly, but made no comment. He likely was wondering how much fire I could produce when needed.

With his arms flung out it looked like the monster was going to grab his intended victims with the claws protruding from his splayed fingers. We stood frozen in place as we watched his werewolf features begin to melt back to human form. I gasped when his head and face came into focus, as if fog had been wiped off a lens. Staring back at us with dead, milky brown eyes was Morgan King, his huge bulk beginning to dissolve into gray ash even as we watched, stunned.

I had never suspected Morgan of anything more than being a crafty used car salesman. His reaction to the beasts seemed as genuine as my own, right down to his chalky white face when he slammed the door on the red-eyed monsters. Now I realized that his fear was not of the beasts, but of my discovery of their secret den. I suppose I was so grateful to have an ally in that putrid smelling pit that I never really questioned his excuse for being down there. Now, I understood that he was probably very worried to be found in such close proximity to the creatures and that helped him to act out his part so convincingly.

Jason was taking my arm and dragging me away from what was left of Morgan's body. The ash was thick on the dirt floor because he was so big in life. I couldn't understand my feelings as I stared, fascinated by the process. I began to feel genuinely saddened with the truth that lay corrupting at our feet.

"Cathleen, let's get out of here. I don't think I can stand on this leg much longer." I heard the pain creeping into his voice and knew if he went down, I'd be hard pressed to get him out of the mine. We never quite turned our backs on the dissolving monster that had once been Jason's friend and someone I had thought of as a harmless, jovial guy. We both brought our own reactions to heel as we labored our way back to the elevator shaft. The ride back up seemed longer and our only comfort was the illumination from the flashlights. I had to close down my fire as it drained my energies too much and I needed that to get us out of there. By the time we reached the top and made our way into the cold air outside the mouth of the mine, the stars and moon were faded completely into the crisp blue of a winter sky.

I got Jason into the car and made sure his wound hadn't started to bleed again. I knew I could deal with it more effectively when we got back to town. Until then, I used a softly spoken charm to close the wound off.

When I got in behind the wheel, I cranked up the heat and shivered in place like a bobble-head doll until I felt some weak warmth creeping out of the vents. I turned to Jason who hadn't spoken since he mentioned his leg to me and broke off my internal dialogue.

Now, he sat stiffly as he had before, cradling his leg with his hands. I reached into my pocket and pulled out the jacket button I'd found in the snow. "Jason," I said, "I found this in the snow when we were looking for the remains of Leo and Jeff."

I handed him the button saying, "Jason, did you suspect Morgan all along?" He turned to me and sighed deeply, turning the gold button over in his hand before answering. "I wasn't sure, but after you two discovered the beasts hidden in WHIP's basement, he began to act like a man with a secret. You know, shifty eyed when I spoke to him and evasive about details surrounding those giant wolves you found. It seemed like he wanted to disassociate himself from that incident."

Turning it over in his hand he said, "This button is off that awful green blazer he always wore." He gave a short, bitter laugh and made a fist over the final piece of the puzzle. "It must have been Morgan who turned Jeff, Cathleen. Jeff just remembered that it was a friend of mine and probably got them mixed up in his head. They were both big guys as kids and Jeff was always the scrawny kid brother we tried to ignore." He stopped speaking and turned his face to the woods as we drove on in silence and thoughts as deep as the forest.

I began to reconstruct things in my mind as we slowly made our way back to town. *Morgan had to have been down in the basement with the monster dogs before he found me down there. I never heard him coming down the stairs and there was no plausible explanation for his being down there in the first place. He'd said he was looking for me so I could close a car deal. Right!*

With the brilliance of hindsight, I now realized how crazy that sounded. It wasn't like I was leaving town with the Jeep. No. It was clear to me now that Morgan was the one feeding the animals penned down there. It was Morgan King who kept them safe from discovery by hiding them in a place no one visited but a few times in the year.

Morgan was well liked and trusted by everyone in Iron Mountain and he carefully used that trust to conceal his dark secrets. *Being a werewolf in a town full of vulnerable humans probably kept that toothy grin on his ugly face,* I thought.

I was getting closer to town when Jason turned to me and said, "Let's go directly to my office, Cathleen. I don't want to run into any folks going over to the Bakery just yet."

A few of the regulars were already lining up outside and scrapping holes in the snow-covered windows to peer into the darkness within. The obvious questions being asked were, "Where is Gus?" and "Why is it still dark inside his shop?"

I slowly drove by and noticed a few folks turning at the sound of the SUV. They recognized it and Jason, and started to cross into the street. "Just keep driving, Cathleen. I don't think I want to answer their questions until I can find a way to do it without sounding totally nuts!"

I waved as we drove on so they wouldn't feel too snubbed and watched their faces in the rear view mirror to try to detect their reaction to our unfriendly behavior. Most just turned back to the shop window to pick up their vigil, but a few stood, staring after the squad car looking bewildered. When we arrived back at the police station, I helped Jason regain his footing and we each carried our shotguns into the chilly office. Jason handed his shotgun to me and asked me to adjust the heat while he went to the back to locate his first aid box. He looked very tired and the stress of the past night was etched on his handsome features. I didn't tell him I had planned to use magic to help heal the gash in his leg. He seemed so exhausted by his grief that I didn't want to give him too many surprises in one day.

I was leaning both guns against the wall next to the thermostat rather than putting them back in the gun cabinet as I thought we'd best keep them close at hand until we sorted this whole thing out. I was getting ready to boost the temperature when I felt a distinctive twitch in my own internal thermometer. I reached back and reclaimed one of the guns from the wall and checked its load automatically.

My skin started to crawl like there was an army of red ants marching across every exposed surface, while a distinctive foul odor seemed to be clinging to the chilled air. My first instinct was to call out to Jason, but with all my senses screaming out a warning I knew I couldn't go rushing to his aid until I was prepared to fight for his life. Was this another of the pack and if so, it was likely someone I knew and because that circle was pretty small, I had only a few names to consider.

Suddenly the fine hairs on the back of my neck began to rise as if in answer to some magnetic pull. My nose was like a bloodhound's on the scent and if I'd had a tail it would have been stiff with expectation. *"Fulla fiada."* I was beginning a silent chant of concealment as I started to move toward the back of the building where the bathroom door was open wide enough to see partially into the interior. That's when I heard the sorrowful sound of a man in pain.

Jason must have switched on the low voltage light that was now swinging from the ceiling like a pendulum on a grandfather clock. But the smell...the smell was all too familiar by now. My body was humming with the power of expectant magic as I watched the sixty-watt bulb make it's back and forth orbit, dimly lighting the interior in the bathroom. My nose literally twitched with an over-load of rotten meat and salivating monster!

That's when I heard something that scared the feathers out of my down vest. "Come on back here, Cathleen! I think the handsome Sheriff may need some of your special attention. Don't be shy now. I'm ready to eat breakfast." The laugh that followed was like the sound of a rabid hyena and I knew Jason and I were on the menu.

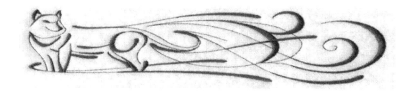

Chapter 32

I scanned what I could see of the room and continued chanting softly as I approached. That's when I saw Jason reflected in the bathroom mirror. He was on the floor, propped against the old-fashioned radiator directly across from the sink. "*Briocht coire.*" My spell began to slow the air down around me causing it to thicken into a heavy, syrupy vapor starting at my feet and rising until it enveloped me.

I knew I was safe inside that seemingly flimsy cocoon, but that didn't reduce the hammering of my heart. Whoever had called my name knew exactly where I was, but didn't show themselves. I didn't have a clue as to their identity from their voice as it seemed distorted, but it sounded indisputably female. That reduced the list of suspects since I only knew a few women and I hated to think who was on that short list.

As I was wracking my brain for names to put with that information on gender, I decided that I needed Jason to be out of the bathroom. I could then attack this creature, whoever they were, without any fear of him being further injured. I called back, "How do I know you haven't already killed the Sheriff? Bring him out here to prove he's still alive...if you're not too afraid of me that is." I threw that in hoping this particular monster was as vain and sure of itself as the others.

I heard a low growl and figured my barb had made its mark on the monster's ego. I was tempted to move forward, but didn't want to be in too narrow a space when I had to confront this being.

Suddenly, there was a wrenching sound as the door to the bathroom was hurled in my direction. I moved back further into the main office carefully keeping my body inside the cocoon. My first thought was that Jason would be the next object hurled out of the room in my direction. As I was preparing myself to grab him if he was, a smoky grey werewolf, the size of the refrigerator exited the bathroom hauling Jason like so much garbage behind its hunched shoulders. It threw him down and Jason landed in an unmoving heap a few feet away.

From where I hovered like a low-flying helicopter, I could see that Jason was bleeding again from his leg and from what I could see, from other places on his torso. His drab brown pants looked saturated and his blood started to pool beneath him. He was pale and his good eye looked glassy and unfocused. *He's in shock from blood loss,* I thought.

Then I turned my attention back to the beast confronting me as it gradually changed forms from a heavily fanged smoky-grey werewolf, into the pretty faced, perky receptionist I knew as Alice.

"Surprise!" she shouted in the direction of my cone of mist. "Bet you never would have guessed that I was one of them would you, Cathleen?" She was smiling like the cat that ate the canary. I didn't answer and she continued. "Well, long story short, I was turned a few years ago by Prescott who promised me eternal youth. I liked the sound of that, but didn't intend to be with Prescott longer than it took me to learn how to dispose of him! I was working on getting the job done before you called to make an appointment to see the old coot. I *persuaded* him to tell you to come for your meeting because I knew about you finding our little darlings in the basement. I figured I wouldn't waste the opportunity and I'd just replace old Prescott with fresh blood--

yours! I never got to finish him off before I had to make a run for it, so to speak."

I wanted to keep her mouth running like a faucet so I could find out if there were others of her kind to be dealt with. I asked "What made you run off before you killed Prescott? He was definitely alone up there when I arrived."

That question seemed to bring out the werewolf in her again as her eyes flashed yellow and her lips were drawing back into a snarl. "That idiot baker came snooping around trying to find you, Cathleen. He had some stupid idea he could save you, but then he wasn't known for his brains, the ugly wart of a man! I wasted too much time on him and had to get back to Iron Mountain before I could be discovered. I figured you and the Sheriff could take care of the Shaman for me and I could sit out the fight."

"What about Morgan?" I asked.

"Oh, he'd do whatever I told him to do. We had our own plans and lots of potential pack members." She was nudging Jason's still body with a toe as if reminiscing, a dreamy look coming over her face. She pushed her long blond hair back over her shoulder as nonchalantly as if we were having a cup of tea together. "I loved being turned by the way. Actually, I became one of the Shaman's favorites because of my special talent for finding new pack members. I didn't need that fussy old Prescott that's for sure." She gurgled out what she probably believed to be a charming giggle.

My words were muffled because of the cone, but she clearly understood them. "I wondered how Morgan was able to access the basement at the station on a regular basis. Guess you've answered that question."

She smiled coyly and I could see long incisors begin to poke out of her pert, pink mouth. "I understand from the Sheriff after some *close questioning* you might say, that I'm the last of the pack," she was saying. "That's alright as I've had my eye on a few of the folks around here who'd be just dandy as my pack subordinates. I must say, Cathleen, I'm impressed by your Celtic ahem...charms! (*Again with that giggle!*) But you might as well drop your attempt at protecting yourself. The Skin Walker taught me some very nasty things when it comes to hurting people."

With that she bent over Jason's still form. She reached down and grabbed a fist full of his thick black hair, pulling on it until his head went back and his arching neck was fully exposed. I saw her body shimmer as if on the brink of turning. I watched as her fingers became claw-like and poised over Jason's jugular. There was no time to think so I reacted like she wanted me to. I shouted my next spell and dissolving the mist that held me safe, I brought up the shotgun I was still clutching at my side and aimed. The sound of the blast took a few seconds to catch up with her movements as she sprang for the door and escape. I was stunned that I missed her at such close range and that she would flee without killing me. Then I saw the trail of dark red blood marking her quick flight. But I couldn't dwell long on the perky little werewolf and quickly knelt down by the unconscious form of the only friend I had left in this town.

I reached out to the healing powers of the winter burdened earth and asked the *Mother* to allow me to absorb the healing energy at the core, below Iron Mountain. My head began to buzz like a thousand bees had invaded it and my hand tightened around Jason's arm. As I crouched by his side, I began to feel a heat coming through the heavy sleeve of his flannel shirt. I felt the deep warmth move over his body like a living thing, passing over him and wrapping around him until his breath came easily and he passed into a deep sleep.

I had no one to help haul him to one of the cell cots so I rolled him onto one of the heavy wool blankets and used it like a sling to drag him closer to the radiator in the office. I placed a pillow under his head and covered him with two other heavy blankets I grabbed out of the cells. After watching him for any signs of reversal in the healing, I allowed myself to sit beside him to regain some spent energy. I guess I hadn't realized how much the healing would take out of me. I performed one last ward to protect Jason while he slept unprotected beside me. I knew he'd not wake for several hours and I didn't have the time to waste waiting for him to regain consciousness.

Alice was on the run and I needed to get her before she disappeared into the forests around Iron Mountain. She was familiar with the dark forests and could lose herself in them for as long as the mountains stood.

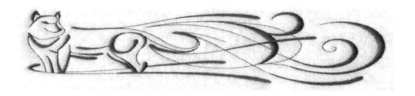

Chapter 33

It was reasonable that there might just be one or two places she'd run to if she wanted to begin making newly minted pack members; her pack members. She likely wouldn't want to spend the long winter days and nights by herself up on Iron Mountain. And since the old mine was off limits to her, she'd be hard-pressed to establish a new den for herself and her victims. Having a few werewolves to help her establish her territory would be a top priority.

The radio station was high on the short list of places she could go with relative impunity. I didn't think she'd leave town without trying to turn a few coworkers to protect her cute and now hairy behind. After all, every leader needs subjects and she'd already told me she was quite good at attacking and turning people into pack members. Now the pack would answer to her if she lived that long.

I bundled back up and headed for the door. Before I went outside I took Jason's squad car keys off their usual hook by the door. I knew I'd do better on the roads with his heavy vehicle and besides, mine was buried under an avalanche of snow at the moment.

The roads were still treacherous, but I didn't have that far to drive so I guessed I had ten minutes to formulate a plan to take down what was hopefully, the last of the Shaman's pack. I mentally went through my wards, charms, spells and chants that might cover such a challenge. I felt frustrated and rather concerned until my mind focused on a specific occasion from my childhood.

We had been up in the mountains near my home doing what my father called "Martial Arts Magic". This form of training consisted mostly of me being thrown to the ground by unseen forces and my father laughing merrily and saying witty things like, "Don't let the faeries hear you cry, Cathleen. They only enjoy themselves all the more!"

I was actually quite good at using my magic to trounce on unsuspecting creatures like cats and dogs until I used it on a skunk and caused my father to move like the wind with me close at his heels. I was less successful at immobilizing prey or creatures bent on evil doings. So now, as I drove carefully over to WHIP Radio, I practiced the only spell that I was sure of, turning a heart inside out. I was certain that Alice still had a heart, even werewolves had hearts. I had to be able to visualize my prey and I wasn't sure what form she'd be in until it dawned on me that she had to be the Alice everyone loved and trusted, or they'd never get near her.

Coming into the station's parking lot I saw only three cars there. One vehicle belonged to my secretary, Darla. The truck belonged to Felix my head engineer, and the SUV belonged to Alice. I prayed to the goddess that she hadn't attacked my staff and left me with three hearts to break.

After looking quickly into the front seat of her car, I knew Alice was still bleeding and hoped she was getting weaker by the minute. I went around to the back entrance just off the basement. That's when I heard the scream. It was a woman's. Darla! It was a sure bet Felix would not have heard as he was likely in the engineering office with headphones, blocking all outside noise.

Another scream. Then, what sounded like furniture being tossed about. I sprinted to the front lobby where I saw Darla being dragged by her hair back to Alice's desk area. She was unconscious, but still breathing.

"Hey there, Alice," I said as cheerfully as I could to mask the fear coursing through me. "Looks like we meet on my turf now. Shall we talk about this while you let Darla go and live to do human things like falling in love and having a real life?"

Alice left the unconscious body of her coworker lying across her desk, but I noticed that she'd turned Darla's head so that her neck was exposed and vulnerable. I didn't like the looks of that.

I began my Celtic spell in a most unusual way. I sang it like an Irish limerick, "ai-thri-och-tru," I crooned in a high, piercing voice.

The five important rhyming lines were of my own devising and I had used this very same to demonstrate to my father how dark witches could be undone by it, enough to find the chink in their armor of spells.

It cut through the air like a speeding bullet and I saw Alice's eyes widen in surprise. That momentary lapse in her control gave me what I needed, the beat of her heart. I now switched to a deep, commanding voice and caused her eyes to roll back in her head. I could see her struggling to tap into her werewolf nature, and there was a momentary flicker of fur and fangs starting to form, but I held her in my spell.

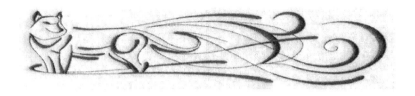

Chapter 34

I cut through Alice's werewolf defenses and exposed her beating heart to my spell. Within a blink of her big blue eyes her warped human heart turned itself inside out. I watched, fascinated, as her face and body flowed back and forth from human to werewolf proving there was still a breath of life in the evil that possessed her. But very soon, this too faded and she fell to the floor, a broken doll.

I became aware that Darla was beginning to stir and when she saw me standing over her, she grabbed for my arms and began to babble incoherently about monsters and demons and Alice turning into a creature who was going to kill her. I did my best to quiet her and then resorted to a spirit calming charm under my breath which fortunately took immediate effect.

Darla looked over at the body of our receptionist sprawled across the floor and burst into tears. This was a better reaction than her talking about monsters. I had to stop her story right now before others heard it. I thought fast.

"Darla," I said soothingly, "I found out a while ago that Alice had a very troubled life and she could act out in violent ways if provoked."

Darla looked back at me with the fear still clearly written on her face and said "The only thing I said to her was "Good morning!"

"Guess she didn't feel like it was a good morning, sweetie, and took it out on you," I answered.

"But she looked horrible, like a monster!" I took a long breath to compose the biggest fib yet. "She suffered from a genetic disorder that affected her skin and hair and her fits of violent temper triggered the physical changes you saw. It's really so sad. Her whole family suffered the same thing."

This seemed to suffice and I added, "Darla, let's respect the memory of the Alice we used to know and not share this story with anyone else. I think she deserves to be remembered as the sweet girl she was under--"

"The Hair!" Darla interjected loudly.

"No, Darla, under the circumstances."

"Oh, sure," she said

After covering Alice with a cheerful tablecloth we found in the lunch room, I told her we'd call the Sheriff as soon as we checked in on Felix.

The *Mother* was smiling upon me as Felix was in good spirits and working away like a little coffee swilling beaver when I poked my head in. "I can't believe you're here, Felix! The roads are really very bad!"

"No sweat, boss. I have a 4 x 4 like you. Got it two years ago from Morgan and what a deal he gave me!"

I told both of my employees to go home after explaining the same story about our receptionist to a stammering Felix. I did add that Alice's heart was very weak and the extreme behavior she displayed toward Darla triggered what I suspected was a massive heart attack. Boy was I good at spinning the yarn!

"I can't believe this, boss. It's like some kind of Twilight Zone re-run!" Felix was saying as he gazed down on the flowered tablecloth that covered Alice. I told them both I had called the Sheriff and he asked that they leave for home immediately so he could remove their co-worker without distressing them further. They both were grabbing for coats and boots before I finished this latest fib.

After I knew I was alone with her body, I uncovered Alice's stiffening corpse and saw she had begun the process of turning to ash as her feet and legs had already dissolved into narrow piles . Spreading the flowery cloth out, I used my hands in rolling motions until the rest of her along with the ash was wrapped tightly inside this make-shift shroud and tied it off so none of the black soot could leak out.

The radio station was surrounded by woods and continuing my hand motions I moved her over the snow and as far into the trees as I could go. With my *green fire* not really a good option as it might be seen in the darkness of the clustered trees, I called for the *Mother* to open the frozen, snow packed ground and remove the evil from this realm. The earth trembled slightly and with a heavy shutter, swallowed what I hoped was the last of the Skin Walker's pack.

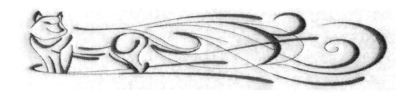

Chapter 35

The tentative light of predawn was beginning to penetrate my consciousness when I became aware of hammering on the front door. We'd both slept through the rest of yesterday and waking up in a new day didn't surprise me. I knew Jason was still healing and I was completely depleted by that healing charm I'd used and my destruction of Alice the Werewolf. I had returned to the Police Station after dispatching Alice and called Darla. I told her to stay at home for the rest of the week. I figured she'd get her composure back by the start of the new week and the whole incident with our demented receptionist could begin to fade.

I had found Jason still in a deep sleep and decided to extend it so that the healing would be completed without any complications. I was too tempted by his sleeping form not to curl up nearby and let Morpheus wrap his arms around me.

The noise began to rouse Jason as he turned toward the door with the bleary look of someone not quite awake enough to understand his surroundings. He saw me as I jumped up and ran to the window. For some reason, he didn't find it surprising to find me there, or that I wouldn't open the door until I had a good look at the visitor and grabbed one of the shotguns that were lying across his desk.

He must have been more awake than I gave him credit for because he said quietly, "Don't open up until I can get to my desk." I scooted back to where he was before he could reinjure himself trying to stand alone. When I reached for his arm he said,

"Cathleen, I feel pretty good, just stiff from sleeping on the floor. You'll have to tell me how that's possible." He was looking at me with what appeared to be some amazement and deep respect.

When he got back onto his feet he stretched himself and sauntered like his old self over to his desk chair where he landed with a resounding plop! "Hey, Sheriff Tate!" we heard through the door, "

We're thinking something bad happened to Gus Flores 'cause he never showed up at the bakery yesterday or today either! Sheriff? You in there?"

Jason hollered back, "Be right with you, Mr. Frazer. I'm just locking up in here." I remembered Talbot Frazer was the town Historian and if anyone would be curious about local goings-on in Iron Mountain, he would be.

"Jason," I said softly, so as not to give my presence away, "Do you think they are all dead?"

"Looking closely at me he answered, "There's no way we can tell just by looking at people. Guess we'll just have to keep our story to ourselves and keep our eyes open at all times for any signs. We'll need to tell them that Gus and Leo took a long planned trip to Alaska so they could do a trek through that wilderness. I remember Gus telling a few folks around here that he wanted to expand his experience of wilderness travel. It might work.

I must have looked worried and not a little skeptical about this method of protecting ourselves from potential killers, because Jason got up and walked over to me. He then surprised me by putting his arms around me in a rather awkward hug. I knew he wasn't comfortable in the role of a sensitive man, so I really appreciated his effort. He looked down on me and seemed to be searching my face for a clue to my true feelings.

"I'm ok, really, Jason." I disengaged from his arms, regretting having to do so and walked over to pick up the other gun off his desk. Giving it to him I said, "Let's go out there and face whatever is waiting."

With that bold statement I began a soft chant for protection and feeling the power from below my feet begin to channel through my limbs, I opened the door to the numbing cold and fearful future.

Off in the distance, the howl of a wolf went unanswered.

FRANCESCA QUARTO is part of a large Italian family where she discovered early on, that a love of reading was as much a part of her DNA as her mother's skill at baking. Growing up in a house filled with laughter, screaming, banging pots, fighting and loving family bonds, shaped her life and heart.

Having moved from the east coast where she was raised between New York and New Jersey, Francesca left for the mid-west where she spent several years outside the Chicago area raising a family of three children, completing her college degrees and writing introspective poetry like other young mothers.

Francesca has worked in local television, a small city zoo, founded a non-profit tutoring agency for an inner-city neighborhood which eventually served local school districts, worked for an International Evangelical Television and Radio Station and for a non-profit organization serving challenged adults.

Francesca Quarto resides in a small town outside of Indianapolis, Indiana with her husband Patrick. She still has a great love of the written word and while she enjoys her E-Reader immensely, she still treasures the excitement of turning the next page.

Tell-Tale Publishing would like to thank you for your purchase. If you would like to read more by this or other fine TT authors, please visit us at: www.tell-talepublishing.com

Made in the USA
Columbia, SC
04 January 2018